MW01113346

WEREWOLF TONIGHT

DON WHITTINGTON lives in Arlington, Texas, with his wife and children. This is his first book for young readers.

Avon Books are available at special quantity discounts for bulk purchases for sales promotions, premiums, fund raising or educational use. Special books, or book excerpts, can also be created to fit specific needs.

For details write or telephone the office of the Director of Special Markets, Avon Books, Dept. FP, 1350 Avenue of the Americas, New York, New York 10019, 1-800-238-0658.

WEREWOLF TONIGHT

DON WHITTINGTON

AN AVON CAMELOT BOOK

If you purchased this book without a cover, you should be aware that this book is stolen property. It was reported as "unsold and destroyed" to the publisher, and neither the author nor the publisher has received any payment for this "stripped book."

WEREWOLF TONIGHT is an original publication of Avon Books. This work has never before appeared in book form. Any similarity to actual persons or events is purely coincidental.

AVON BOOKS
A division of
The Hearst Corporation
1350 Avenue of the Americas
New York, New York 10019

Copyright © 1995 by Don Whittington
Excerpt from *Vampire Mom* copyright © 1995 by Don Whittington
Published by arrangement with the author
Library of Congress Catalog Card Number: 94-96292
ISBN: 0-380-77513-1
RL: 5.2

All rights reserved, which includes the right to reproduce this book or portions thereof in any form whatsoever except as provided by the U.S. Copyright Law. For information address Avon Books.

First Avon Camelot Printing: June 1995

CAMELOT TRADEMARK REG. U.S. PAT. OFF. AND IN OTHER COUNTRIES, MARCA REGISTRADA, HECHO EN U.S.A.

Printed in the U.S.A.

OPM 10 9 8 7 6 5 4 3 2 1

To Adam,
with love as always

1

The fire raged behind, and ahead stood the wizard, his eyes blazing with reflected flame. He held his hands before him, the fingers long and spindly like a spider's legs. He grinned wickedly, then whispered. The words floated toward me on sulphurous breath.

"Die, Chronicler!" A shape reached out for me from the flames . . .

I came to with a small yelp, and sat upright in bed. A dream. It was just a dream. Yet, as I looked across the room and through the windows to the Poe house next door I shivered and wrapped my blankets tight around me.

The Poes were new to our neighborhood, and no one in my family had seen them. Somehow, I was certain that my terrible dream and the house next door were connected. But how?

It was my last free month before sixth grade and it was Friday, my day to do the yard. I dragged myself from bed and put on my oldest blue jeans. As I dressed I kept one eye on the house across the way. Thin curtains covered the windows, and I imagined shapes were moving about behind them.

The moving trucks had arrived the day before, and I had watched, astonished, as all sorts of strange and mysterious things were carried into the house. The furniture was old, and seemed out of place. Huge boxes which might have held anything from phone booths to coffins were carried through the door.

My mother watched, too, and commented on the things going in.

"Oh look, Winston, what a beautiful wardrobe!"

What my mother called a wardrobe looked exactly like a guillotine frame to me. It wasn't long before I realized that she and I were not seeing the same things go inside. I didn't know what that meant. I watched as the movers carried what looked like a mummy's sarcophagus inside.

"They have such lovely furniture," Mom said. "I'm sure they must be wonderful people."

I started to object, but held my silence. If Mom wanted to believe the Poes were ordinary people, then I wasn't going to argue about it. Mom and Dad were convinced I had an unhealthy imagination, anyway.

I walked across the room and began putting the things I'd need for the day in my pockets: a dollar and forty-seven cents left from my allowance, my jack-knife, and my lucky agate marble. In the bathroom I ran a comb through my hair quickly, then jumped three steps at a time down the stairs to breakfast.

Mom and Dad had already gone to work. I slipped frozen waffles into the toaster, and read Mom's note.

Don't forget it's yard day. Do me a favor and slip the clothes from the washer into the dryer later. If you go somewhere, leave us a note. Be careful with the lawnmower.

Love, Mom

Mom was a great believer in notes. Even though I'd done the yard every Friday all summer, she always thought she had to remind me.

Over waffles I glanced through the paper looking for new movies. It was disappointing. I'd already seen all the horror movies I could sneak out of the video store (my mom didn't approve) and all the new ones playing in town. I sighed. Well, there was always the yard.

By the time the grass was mowed and I'd finished with the weed-whacker it was lunch time. I put the tools away, and set the sprinkler.

Satisfied with the yard, I started practicing with my slingshot. It was a special model, made for competition, with a padded fore-arm brace, and thick springy elastic that could send a rock or a ball bearing over two hundred feet with accuracy. I'd won first place in my age group during last spring's competition, and I had no intention of losing my title in the next tournament.

Dad had fixed up a practice area for me near the fence, and I'd set the sprinklers so that area remained dry. I arranged my cans and began knocking them over from about fifty feet away. It's a nice feeling to be good at something, and I took great satisfaction in my skill.

I'd been practicing about twenty minutes when someone spoke.

"You're pretty good at that."

The voice startled me. I turned to find a kid looking at me over the chain link fence. He was shorter than I, and plump, almost round. His hair was jet black, swept back straight as if painted on his skull. His hairline came down on his forehead in a *V*. He wore a t-shirt with broad stripes that made him look even fatter, and a pair of dark pants.

"Who are you?" I asked.

He blinked slowly, like a frog. "My name is Brock. Brock Lee Poe."

I grinned. "Broccoli?"

He blinked again. "My friends call me Broccoli. You can, if you wish."

"I'm Winston."

"I know," he said. "Why don't you come over?"

I pointed at the house. "You're one of my new neighbors?"

"Yes. I arrived last night." I still didn't much care

4

for the feeling that house gave me, but meeting Broccoli made things a little better. After all, he was just another kid. How strange could things be over there when they had a kid? Besides, I was burning up with curiosity about their place.

"Okay," I said. I put my slingshot and targets away while he watched. I climbed over the fence, and we walked up the steps to his back porch. "Do you play Nintendo?"

"No. I'm not very interested in video games."

"Oh," I said, beginning to regret I'd come over. What kind of kid doesn't like video games? "What do you want to do then?"

"Something better," he said. His eyes were a deep black, but within them some bright power seemed to burn. I was held by them. "Do you like spooky stuff?" he asked me.

"Are you kidding? Who doesn't?"

"Good. I thought you might. So why don't we do something . . . spooky?"

"Like what?" I asked.

He gave me a mysterious smile. "I thought we might have a seance."

I grinned. "Now *that* would be cool. You mean a real seance? Like with dead people? Do you really know how?" I was nervous and excited at the same time. My mom would have a conniption if she knew.

"Of course," he smiled. "After all, a seance with the living would just be a phone call."

I licked my lips. "Let's do it. Who shall we try and talk to? What about Kennedy?"

He held the door open for me. "No. Today I think we'll try and talk to the Amber Man."

"The Amber Man!" I whistled softly. I felt that strange creepiness in my spine that I'd felt when I awoke from my dream. I held back for a moment. I wanted to turn and run as fast as I could back to my house. Then I heard a voice in my head, not the voice of my dream, but a gentler one.

Go with him. You are the Chronicler!

I turned as if I could catch the whisperer behind me, but there was no one. I looked back at Broccoli, grinned half-heartedly, then stepped through Broccoli's back door into another world.

2

Broccoli's house was like a curiosity shop. Strange paintings leaned against empty bookshelves, or sat tilted on massive sofas. Every room we passed through seemed crowded with weird and mysterious things. There were moose heads and shrunken heads and dolls with no heads at all. Shiny, futuristic apparatus stood next to antique kitchen tools. It was a bewildering array of useless things, and I had no idea what to make of it all.

"Where are your folks?" I asked.

"Working."

"What do they do?"

"They're scientists. They work for Time." Broccoli led me into their kitchen. "Want some lunch?"

"Sure. What have you got?"

"Anything you want."

"Okay, a cheeseburger."

"Done." Broccoli punched buttons on a bizarre looking microwave, and opened the door. He handed me a fresh cheeseburger. The chamber inside the oven was empty. I frowned as he shut the door and punched more buttons. Then he opened the door again and took out a hot dog for himself.

"What the . . ."

He sat down and began to eat. "It's an electronic chef. From the twenty-first century."

"Oh, sure. Twenty-first century. Of course." I bit into the cheeseburger. It was pretty good.

"Uh-huh," he said. He reached behind him, opened the refrigerator, and snagged us each a Dr Pepper.

"This is the twentieth century, you know."

He shrugged. "I told you my folks worked for Time."

"I thought you meant *Time* magazine."

"No, they work for Time, Incorporated. It's a late twenty-first century company. They travel all over. I can show you the cabinet. It's in the study."

"Cabinet?"

"The time cabinet. The transporter." Broccoli looked disappointed. "You can't tell me all these concepts are unfamiliar to you."

"Hey, it isn't every day someone claims to be from the future."

"Oh, I'm not from the future. I was born eleven years ago. But my folks are from the future."

"Oh, well then. I understand everything." He was beginning to annoy me.

"No. No, I don't think you do. But you will."

We finished our sandwiches in silence, and I had to admit to myself that even though what he said couldn't be true and he was pretty strange, the whole thing was at least interesting.

Broccoli took a swig from his soda. He wiped his mouth with the back of his hand. "Do you know about the Amber Man?"

"Sure. Everybody knows about him."

The Amber Man had been big news for months. He made the cover of all the magazines, and was often featured on the television news. Last April a group of cavers in France came across an amber vein at the corner of a huge underground cavern. Sealed within the freakish gem was a man from the fourteenth or fifteenth century.

It was an incredible scientific find. The preservative nature of the amber had kept the man intact. Scientists were anxious to free him from the amber and study everything about him, from his physical structure to the things in his pockets.

"Did you know he's in London now?" Broccoli asked.

"No, I didn't. Why?"

"Seems they have a better lab than the one in Paris. They're going to cut him free of the amber with precision laser scalpels. They'll remove it a micron at a time.''

"They can do that?''

"It seems so. You finished? I'll show you the study.''

"Yeah, sure,'' I said, and knocked back the rest of the soda. I followed Broccoli through the living room to the study. It was a huge room with tall shelves lining three walls. In one corner was a large cabinet that emitted a faint glow. To the side were numbers and letters reading "Philadelphia, April 5, 1776.''

I chuckled looking at it. It was like something out of a bad science fiction film. Heck, the letters and numbers weren't even in a panel. Someone appeared to have painted them on. I wondered what kind of game Broccoli was playing.

As if he could read my mind, Broccoli pointed to the sign. "You've noticed the display,'' he said. "This ought to convince you.'' He held his hand below the sign and suddenly the letters began to merge and change. The shifting stopped at "Moscow, December 9, 1864.'' I stepped forward and touched the letters.

There was no hint of any mechanical device. There were no knobs, no plates, no touch panels, no keys. And had I not seen them change I would have sworn the letters were printed on the side of the cabinet.

"That's pretty slick,'' I admitted. "What is it? Some kind of hologram?''

He gave me a secretive smile. "Something like that.''

10

I began to pay more attention. To the side of the cabinet there was a chest of drawers. One drawer was open and filled with several, rather plain looking talismans on chains. I hefted one in my palm. It was pretty light.

"Those are translators," Broccoli said. "Whenever my folks go back they wear these in case the country and time they're visiting speaks a different language, or has different slang than they're used to. It helps them blend in."

"How do they work?"

"I have no idea. C'mon, let's have our seance."

Broccoli led me to a table. It was round and made of dark wood. The letters of the alphabet, and the digits 0 through 9 were worked on small pieces of tile inlaid around the top face of the table. A long arm led from the table center to a round, crystal lens which was currently hovering over the letter *B*.

Broccoli ran his hand across the table and gave the arm a spin. "This is a type of spirit table. My father saved it from the wreckage of Cagliostro's villa. He gave it to me as a present."

"Your father approves of you trying to talk to spirits? Seems kind of funny for a scientist."

Broccoli laughed. "I think he's hoping I'll grow out of it. But I can't help it. I've always thought the supernatural was more interesting than science."

11

"I can't disagree with that," I said. I sat in a chair across from Broccoli. "So how does it work?"

"Usually you collect a circle of ten people who hold hands and address the spirit. If the spirit is summoned, it communicates by moving the lens. It spells out answers to our questions."

"Can we do it with only two?"

Broccoli smiled. "Ordinarily, no. But you're the Chronicler. Between us, we are complete. It will work."

I didn't know what to say. Suddenly the image of the wizard flashed across my mind. I shivered.

The glass lens began to move. A chill breeze stirred through the room, and I could see the curtains begin to flutter as if creatures were stretching behind them. I could hardly breathe.

"Are . . . are you doing that?" I whispered.

Broccoli appeared as surprised as I. "No! I've never seen it move without any summoning before."

The glass spun rapidly through the words. I watched fascinated, spelling the words in my mind. It was easy, almost like reading a book.

I am Sacajawea.

"The Indian?" I asked, surprised.

"She's always been my spirit guide," Broccoli answered in an excited voice. "Who better?"

"Well, if she was good enough for Lewis and Clark—"

The danger is too great.

12

Broccoli frowned. "What danger? We want to talk to the Amber Man."

Suddenly, the hand stopped spinning, and a spectral voice filled the room.

You must not.

"Why? What's the problem?" Broccoli took the voice in stride, as if disembodied voices were perfectly normal.

He is in thrall to the evil one. He seeks you now!

"What evil one? What on earth are you talking about?"

Radoul. It is Radoul. Even now I struggle to keep him at bay. You are the Key, the Chronicler is with you. Together you must stop them.

"Who?" My voice was as high as a girl's.

Those who would awake the Amber Man. He must not be freed.

"Why?"

Werewolf!

"But . . ." Before Broccoli could speak there came a crackling pop and an odor of sulphur tinged the air even as the lens began to spin at terrific speed.

Fools! You seek the Amber Man. See, he is here!

The air above the table turned dark and wisps of smoke rose from the board. The tendrils coalesced until the figure of a man began to form. But this was like no man I'd ever seen. His eyes blazed red and tears of blood ran down his face. His jaws jutted from his face and fangs caught the light, reflected it like diamonds. Saliva dripped from him and hit my arm. It stung like fire!

The beast twirled to stare at Broccoli who was frozen with terror. The wolf floated above the table roaring in fury, the sound loud enough to hurt my ears. I could hear the hum of the time cabinet. I glanced behind me. The letters on the transporter whirred crazily. I returned my attention to the table. I tried to concentrate through the noise and terror. The spirit spoke.

Broccoli, you must run. Flee through the cabinet. The beast cannot harm the Chronicler. Run for your very soul!

Broccoli gave no sign he heard. His eyes were captured by the hateful glare of the werewolf.

"Broccoli!" I screamed. "Run, now. Sacajawea says you must escape through the cabinet. Hurry, before it's too late. He can't harm me."

He seemed bolted to the chair. His eyes were spread wide and remained fixed on the werewolf which now began to bend as if to take him in its paws. Without thinking, I reached over and threw my arms around the werewolf's legs. It was there, but it wasn't. I could feel its stiff hair, could smell the sour stench of its hide, and some other, earthy smell like the grave. But I was holding nothing, only air. The creature hesitated, turned to glare at me, and at last Broccoli found his wits.

14

"Run, Broccoli!" I yelled, and Broccoli moved.

He scrambled from his chair just as the werewolf reached for him. With a terrified yell he sped across the room and leaped into the cabinet. Again the werewolf screamed, but this time his fury had no target. I let go and a blast of force threw me across the room where I slammed into the wall. I could still smell him. He glared at me, made several motions as if to leave the table. Finally he pointed one claw at me and snarled. Then he was gone.

It took me a while to get my breath. Everything had happened so fast. I stood carefully. Nothing was broken. The lens was spinning. The voice of the spirit came again.

Winston, Winston, Winston.

"I'm here," I said, still panting. I touched the burning place on my arm. "You said he couldn't hurt me."

Only psychic pain. You have no burn. You are of this world. He could not touch you. Broccoli is only partly of your world. He is . . . the spirit seemed to hesitate *. . . another kind of thing.*

"Whatever."

You must follow.

"You're nuts." I glanced in fear at the cabinet. Everything Broccoli had said was true. He'd vanished inside that cabinet. It wasn't a game anymore. Time travel was real.

15

It is your destiny. You are the Chronicler.

"I am not! I'm just a kid who lives next door to some . . . some kind of nut. I won't go."

Then he will die.

I hung my head, and brushed back tears. *Or I will,* I thought, remembering my dream. An odor of fresh pines and high mountains filled the room. I looked up. Again an image formed above the table, only this time it was a woman. Her face was slender, her hair long. She was dressed in hides. She looked around the room. She held a hand before her and pointed.

There, she said in a ghostly voice. I walked to where she pointed and picked up a belt.

"This?"

She nodded. *You will need it to get back. Broccoli knows how to use it. He is the Key. Take the talismans as well. You will need them.*

I stood holding the belt, trying to decide. Sacajawea smiled.

You have great strength of heart. You will decide well. Good speed, Chronicler. And then she vanished.

I waited another moment, then began to strap on the belt. I sighed deeply. This was the craziest thing I had ever done. I grabbed two talismans, and slipped them both around my neck. I walked to the cabinet. I laughed as the thought of leaving a note suddenly crossed my mind.

Dear Mom,
I've gone through time to fight a werewolf. Back for supper.

Winston

I stopped laughing, held my breath, and stepped through. The last thing I saw was the sign: "France, May 12, 1429"!

3

A strange tingling ran through my body as I stepped through the cabinet. Before I could get used to it, I popped out next to Broccoli. He and I stepped almost simultaneously onto soft green grass. We were startled by a cry from behind us.

Broccoli and I spun to face a warrior. He moved swiftly in chain armor, and swung a broadsword through the air. His face was set in stern lines as he eyed us.

"Speak!" he barked. "Are you spirits from God, or demons? For if you be the devil's breed I shall carve you beneath God's sun no matter your powers!"

The warrior's ferocity took me by surprise. I forgot Broccoli wasn't wearing a translator. He hadn't understood a word. He snatched at one of the talismans about my neck, and I quickly whipped it over my head and around his.

"We're not demons, and we're not spirits. We're kids," I said nervously, my eyes on the sword.

18

"Right," said Broccoli. Now that he wore the talisman he could keep up.

"Do not lie. I saw you step from the very ether as through a doorway."

Something about the voice caught my attention. I looked again at the face. I gasped, "You're a girl!"

"Aye, and what business is that of yours. I am Joan of Arc, General of the armies of France, liberator of Orleans, servant to Almighty God and the Dauphin of France. Provoke me at your peril!"

"Joan of Arc! Holy cow!" I said.

Her eyes narrowed. "What is this blasphemy? Are you pagans? Do you worship beef?"

Broccoli had regained control of himself. He stepped forward cautiously, his hands spread, palms wide.

"Nay, we are not pagans. He muttered what is but a mild oath in our land. We beg your pardon, great General." My eyes widened at the fancy speech.

Joan listened, but she kept her weapon at the ready. For the first time I noticed that her sword arm was wounded. She was only about seventeen, and not much bigger than I. How she could hold that heavy sword at all, much less with a wounded arm, was beyond me.

"And where would be your land?" she asked.

"The kingdom of Prester John," Broccoli said. This was news to me. I had never heard of such a place. It was the right answer, though, for slowly she lowered her sword.

"I have heard often of the godly kingdom of Prester John, of the good works and miracles done in God's name there. Yet there are those who say it is but a myth, and that such magic cannot be."

"Yet you see us before you," said Broccoli calmly. I began to relax.

"True. Indeed, who but the monks of Prester John could appear from the air as you have done? Still, you seem young and strangely garbed to be monks."

Broccoli bowed. "As you seem young and female to be a general."

Joan colored as if angry, then smiled slowly. She drove her sword into the ground. "By the Dauphin, that is well said, and true." She chuckled, outright. She held out her hand, and clasped Broccoli's arm in hers, hands up to the elbows. "Be welcome in my camp." She turned and took my arm in the same fashion.

"Come with me," she said. "We do not have much; armies on the move never do. But we can give you a meal, and a place to sleep tonight. Perhaps you can tell us of your travels, and what brings you to France in such grave times."

We followed her from the grove down a narrow trail through dense forest. The darkness beneath the canopy of leaves made it difficult to judge the time of day. I needed to talk to Broccoli, but he marched happily along at Joan's heels, and I had no chance.

We emerged into a huge encampment spread wide

over a lush valley. Crude tents were struck everywhere, and the air was thick with smoke and the smell of waste. I wrinkled my nose. Groups of men stood at attention as we walked by. Joan gave little notice of them, but I saw the fierce pride and loyalty shining in their eyes as they watched her.

We came to a large tent near the center of the camp, and Joan led us inside. She spoke to a soldier at the entrance.

"See these guests are brought wine, and food if they're hungry. Send a messenger to de Bandricourt to meet me in the command tent." The soldier bowed, and sped away.

Joan turned to us. "You will please me by staying here until we decide what to do with you."

"Are we prisoners?" I asked, worried.

She looked at me with thoughtful eyes. "No, not prisoners. But these are times of war, and we do not accept guests without precautions. Make yourselves comfortable until I send for you."

With that, she turned and left the tent, leaving Broccoli and me alone.

"I'd like to go home now, please," I said.

"We can't," said Broccoli. "Not until we destroy the werewolf." He lay down on a mat of straw and closed his eyes.

A man stuck his head inside the tent. "Do you require food?" he asked.

"We just ate," I answered. As he left I muttered, "Yeah, we just had lunch five hundred and sixty-four years from now!" I walked to a pile of straw and spread it out on the cold ground. Broccoli was already asleep. I lay down, and yawned. Something about time travel must have worn me out, because in moments I drifted away.

⌃4⌃

I awoke with a vague feeling of unease. I opened one eye and saw someone bending over Broccoli. The figure was murmuring as its head swung from side to side.

> *"None's to left, none's to right;*
> *Dabble's deeds is out of sight!"*

He laughed softly, and reached toward Broccoli. I gasped, and his hand stopped, hovering over Broccoli as he turned. It was then I saw the glint of his knife blade.

He looked like a monkey, all wrinkled with nose and eyes and lips too close together in a wide, white plate of face. His tiny ears stuck out to either side like delicate knobs. He snarled at me, revealing tiny needle teeth.

> *"Some's woke up to sees the light;*
> *Dabble puts it out, all right!"*

23

He lunged for me. I yelled and twisted off the straw. From the corner of my eye I saw Broccoli's hand whip out to trip the man who fell on his hideous face with a surprised yelp.

Broccoli leaped to his feet, and together we burst through the tent flap with Dabble right behind us. We got less than ten yards before the guards seized us and held us still.

"What's going on?" said an angry voice.

Three soldiers had hold of Dabble who was spitting and snarling like an animal. The soldiers holding Broccoli and me relaxed as they watched.

"That man tried to kill us," said Broccoli.

"Let me go you stinking goatses;
Dabble's got to cuts they throatses."

The soldiers got the knife away from him, and bound his hands behind him. Dabble continued to struggle, his tiny eyes sparking like flints. I shuddered.

"The Maid requests your presence," a soldier said, addressing Broccoli. "I am Nen, Captain of the Guard. Perhaps the Maid can take the measure of this mischief. Keep that—that creature under guard until I send for you," he said to the soldiers around Dabble.

The guards released us, and we followed warily. It was good to get away from Dabble, whatever kind of man he was. Just the same, I was anxious about our fate at Joan's hands. What if she thought we were spies?

Nen led us inside the large command tent. At a table sat Joan of Arc surrounded by soldiers—her commanders I presumed. Nen brought them up to date about our encounter with Dabble.

Joan snapped at us. "What do you know about this man?"

"Nothing, I assure you," said Broccoli. "I was astonished to awake and find him over me with a knife. Had it not been for the quick wits of my friend he'd have cut my throat."

It was the first I'd heard of any quick-witted action on my part, but I blushed as Joan eyed me with new appreciation.

A large man to Joan's left asked, "What is your purpose here?"

Broccoli bowed. "Our purpose is somewhat muddled in that we have only a name to go by. We seek one named Radoul."

A hush fell over the tent. The tall man's face grew grave, and one or two of the men seemed to pale.

"What is it, Captain? This name means something to you?" asked Joan.

"You have not heard of Baron Radoul, the Blood Baron of Jura?"

Joan smiled wryly. "You forget, Captain de Bandricourt, that before you escorted me to the Dauphin I was but a peasant girl. I know little of barons or other nobility.''

''A baron he may be, but I think there is more nobility in a serpent than in Radoul.'' De Bandricourt spit, and made a sign against the evil eye.

At that moment, the captain of the guard reentered. ''General, the villain has escaped.''

''What? How is that possible? Were you not watching him?''

''Aye, sweet Maid, three men had him under lock and key. Yet, he vanished into the very ground like a mole.''

''That's impossible,'' said de Bandricourt.

''Look,'' I shouted, pointing. A mound of earth shuddered beneath the tent wall and suddenly the creature burst before us, arms spread, his fingers splayed in bone-hard blades like picks.

> *''Armies keeps us not apart;*
> *Dabble plucks his nasty heart!''*

Like lightning the creature's hand shot toward Broccoli's chest. Broccoli winced, and moved back as an arc of silver sliced through the air and chopped Dabble's hand from his arm. Thick, black liquid oozed from his stump. Dabble hissed as if it smarted no more than a paper cut. The severed hand lay flexing on the ground.

Joan faced the creature, her eyes burning, her blade soiled with the black bile of Dabble's blood.

"By the visions of St. Michael, St. Margaret, and St. Catherine who guide me, I command you. What manner of being are you? Speak."

Dabble stared thoughtfully at the end of his arm, then snarled at Joan.

"Dabble makes no idle boast;
The heretic Joan of Arc will roast!"

Her face blazed in fury. She thrust her sword and stabbed him through the heart. Dabble sucked in his breath; his face began to move as if the muscles beneath his skin were going crazy. He threw back his head and howled. His body shivered and the flesh began to creep and crawl across his bones. He turned scarlet, then black as his body seemed to melt, and mold in upon itself. He transformed into hundreds of snakes which fell hissing into the hole he'd made as they slithered off the sword.

Watching them, I felt a stab of queasy fear. "What the heck have I got into?" I whispered.

Beside me Broccoli knelt as the last of the snakes—which a moment before had been the severed hand—slipped into the hole, vanishing beneath the earth. Joan trembled, moaning with horror and disgust. She bowed her head, then fell to her knees in prayer.

I stood helplessly as, one by one, the men dropped

to pray in whispers all around me. For the first time it hit me that what Broccoli and I had stumbled into was real—and dangerous.

All I could think of was home, and my parents and that I'd only met Broccoli the day before and found myself in this mess. I remembered the light spray of sprinklers in the warm sun, the scent of fresh cut grass. I wanted to cry, but I could not. Too much was happening, and happening too fast for me to do more than roll with it.

Finally Joan rose. She gazed at me. "We commend you to your quest. Go with our good will and our prayers. Such evil as this must be met and matched. Perhaps the monks of Prester John are up to such a task. I do not envy you. For our part, we will provide you with a guide to take you across country to Jura. It is little enough, but we are at war and can spare no more." She turned to de Bandricourt.

"Captain, find one among the men familiar with the mountains, someone from that region. Seek a volunteer. I will not order a man to travel among such horrors. Find sturdy ponies for these monks, and a week's provisions."

"It is done, my General." De Bandricourt left the tent with the other men.

I turned to Broccoli, who was still on one knee, looking at his ankle.

"Well, at least we'll be able to ride," I said.

"It's just as well," he said. "I've been bitten."

⫷5⫸

A dwarf named Django volunteered to be our guide. We followed him down narrow trails eastward across France. Within three days Broccoli's foot had swelled to twice its normal size. I continued to clean the wound each day and change the dressing, but it was doing little good. Every day he grew weaker as his calf grew blacker, and it was hard for him to travel. But he was tougher than he looked; he would not stop. So we rode on.

Broccoli now wore the belt, the device that would, hopefully, return us to our own time. Its controls were complicated. The first day out of camp he showed me how to operate it, but I didn't understand most of what he said. It was a relief to give it back to him. As for me, I carried nothing more than a bag of medicines, my translator/talisman, and a long dagger which Nen, the Captain of the Guard, had given me.

The days dragged long and dull with the endless clopping of our horses, and Broccoli's condition worsened with every mile. For such a rough looking man, Django was amazingly gentle with him, helping him with his pony, and making his bed comfortable at night. Around the campfire the little soldier's eyes shone as he told us about Joan of Arc and the Battle of Orleans.

"She was a lion, more fierce than any of our men. Who can doubt she walks with God? Her captains fought her at every turn, resented her, doubted her." He grinned with satisfaction. He thumped his chest. "But I never doubted her. I knew she would win. Now, they all know!"

Broccoli fidgeted under his blanket. He moved his leg trying to ease the pain. "Do you know this man we're trying to find, Django?"

The dwarf frowned, and his features seemed to deepen as if he were regarding a great injustice.

"I know him." He spit into the flames. "Were his evil not balanced by the Maid of Orleans I would declare the world a wasteland and tear out my heart."

"You've actually met him, then?" I asked.

"I was his Hop-frog," he muttered, his voice bitter. "He kept me to amuse him. I played the jester, the fool." Django looked at me. The fire's smoke waved before him like a cobra. "But he was the fool. He kept nothing from me. I saw him as he practiced his dark arts, watched him torture and kill. And all the time he didn't care what I saw."

30

"Why not?"

"Would you keep secrets from a dog? I was no more to him. He thought I could not learn, you see. But I did learn. I watched, and listened, and when the chance came to escape I took it."

"And now you're going back."

He shrugged. "The Maid has asked it of me. I will not deny her." He pulled his sword, held it glinting in the firelight. "Less than a dog, he thought of me. But after all, even dogs can bite. Perhaps Radoul will learn that frogs can bite, too."

At the mention of biting, I went over to Broccoli. I unwrapped his bandage.

"You just did that," he said. His flesh burned my fingers.

"I'm doing it again," I said through clenched teeth. "You have fever." A horrible odor rose from the wound, which had turned black around the edges. "It's getting worse."

I cleaned the wound with herbed water, and wrapped it again with a fresh bandage from my bag. "At this rate, I'll be out of bandages in another day."

"At this rate, I'll be dead in two days," he mumbled weakly.

"If you had a doctor . . ."

"You saw what happened back there. A doctor can't help me, and you know it. It's some kind of magic, a spell." Broccoli bit his lip. "There's something I'm

31

missing—an idea—if only it wasn't so hard to think."
He closed his eyes, and lay back shivering. I tucked the
blanket tightly around him and returned to the fire.

Django was cutting at a piece of birch.

"He needs help," I said.

Django nodded. "I thought so, myself." His head
jerked up. "What was that?"

He looked out into the trees.

A pair of eyes stared in at us. Django held the sword
before him, and I felt my own hand reaching for the
dagger in my waistband.

For a moment nothing moved. Then slowly the eyes
came closer as, with a curious rocking motion, the thing
approached the fire. I relaxed.

"It's just a rabbit," I said. But Django put a warning
hand on my arm. His eyes stayed fixed on the rabbit.

"Not a rabbit, a hare. And no normal hare, either.
Since when did a hare approach a fire?"

It stared at us, its nose twitching. Its eyes were dis-
concerting. They had an intelligent, malevolent quality.
The animal lifted its head, its huge ears folding against
the ground behind it, and howled. My heart froze at the
horrible, ululating scream that ripped through the forest,
and even Django shrank backward in fear. Then like a
flash, the hare was gone, leaving us trembling and alone
in the silent darkness.

For what seemed an eternity, I could not move.
Django leaped to his feet shouting, "The ponies!"

32

I scrambled up beside him. We ran to where we'd left our steeds. They were gone. The scream had driven them frantic, caused them to tear free of their ground reins and flee. Django cursed as he called in vain for the ponies. At last there was nothing for it, but to return to camp.

My spirits were as low as they could go. Why was this happening to me? This was supposed to be an adventure, but it was all going wrong.

"What are we going to do?" I wailed. "The ponies are gone, and Broccoli can't walk."

"It doesn't matter," he said, in a choked voice. "Look."

I whimpered as I saw the spear thrust through the bedroll into the ground beneath.

"No, no! Broccoli!" I ran to the bedroll, grabbed the spear and pulled it free. I fell to my knees and threw back the blanket.

Broccoli had vanished!

6

It was all just too much. I sank to my knees and cried like a baby. Broccoli was gone, taken who knows where; our horses were run off; and I was stuck in fifteenth century France with a dwarf named Django and no way home.

Django ignored me. I watched through tears as he examined Broccoli's bedroll and searched for signs of our attacker's passing. I didn't care. I wanted to go home. I picked up a dirt clod and threw it against a tree. Django spun at the noise, sword out, then glared at me. He went back to his searching, and I continued to weep.

After a bit, I looked up and saw him hunkered before me. He offered me a bowl of broth. "Drink this," he said.

I took the bowl, and sipped. It was bitter, but it was hot, and somehow soothing. Django watched me, and I took comfort in the fact that an adult was around. In

my fear and self-pity I'd somehow slipped into an auto-
matic kid mode. Let the adults handle things, that's the
ticket. It shamed me.

"You're no monk," said Django. "No monk of Prester John would be so weak."

"I don't even know who Prester John is," I
whispered.

Django sighed. "I doubt he exists. I think he is a
story the priests tell to keep us from fearing the pagans
in the east. Prester John is supposed to be king of a
Christian kingdom in the Orient."

I shook my head. "I'm pretty sure there was never
anybody like that," I said.

" 'Was.' I thought so. You are from the future,
aren't you?"

I stared at him in surprise. "How . . . ?"

"Do not presume that people who know less than
you are stupid or are you so advanced in your time that
I am just an idiot to you?" Despite his words his face
showed amusement.

"No, I never meant—"

"No, people never do. But it's so, isn't it. You are
from the future. A time filled with miracles, no doubt,
and filled with people of great beauty and wisdom." He
laughed. "Nevertheless, I think I prefer my own time
to yours. At least we do not hide from what we must
do. Crying is no substitute for action."

"That's easy for you to say. You're a soldier. You're

35

used to all this. You're strong. I'm just a kid. I don't even know Broccoli very well. I'm not supposed to be here.''

Django gripped my shoulders, drew my face close to his. His brown eyes seemed to glow in the firelight.

''We are all who we are, in whatever time. What counts, what makes us what we are is *why* we are here. No man is strong unless he has a cause. It is purpose that defines our strength, nothing more. The Maid of Orleans is only a child, yet she leads all the army of France against the hated English, and she wins! Why? Because her arms are thicker than English arms, her legs more powerful? You've seen her. Does she stand taller? Is she faster? Or perhaps she does not impress you. Perhaps in your time this happens every day.''

''No,'' I whispered.

''She wins because her purpose is true. As our purpose is true. The Blood Baron is evil. He must be taken. Perhaps we can save your friend, perhaps not. Perhaps we can beat the Baron, perhaps not. But we must try, despite our weakness. Are you with me?''

I shuddered. All around us the dark night seemed so forbidding. What could I do? I had no talents. What was *my* purpose? But in the dark curl of smoke from our fire I seemed to see the spirit, Sacajawea, and could hear her voice inside me. *You are the Chronicler; he is the Key. He will die without you!* Django released me. He stood and brooded, mistaking my decision.

36

"So, you are giving up," he said.

"No," I said, rising. "No, I'm not. I don't know what good I can do, but I have to try. I'll never get home if I don't."

Django swelled as if with pride as he looked at me. I was still afraid, but suddenly it was important that he respect me. My hands shook as I gathered my things. I jerry-rigged a backpack and slung it into place. Django stood ready to go.

"I hope you're right. I hope the cause is enough, but I can't think of a single thing I can do that's going to help us. I'm not like Joan of Arc, you know. I'm not that strong."

Django gave a little smile. "Purpose is like a great wind. It carries you forward whether you will it or not. And in a great wind, even a straw can pierce an oak."

" 'Great. Now I'm a straw. Well, as a great man once said, 'Wet's get that wascally wabbit!' "

Django frowned. "Is that from your time?"

"Uh, yeah. It's Elmer Fudd."

Django nodded. He drew his sword and started into the dark forest. As he walked he said, "He must indeed be a great philosopher. I'm sure I don't understand it."

"You have to see the cartoon," I said. I followed him into the darkness.

37

7

The way through the woods was black and the sliver of moon above did nothing to help us. I grimaced as wisps of leaf and vines brushed my face and hands like cobwebs. Django had eyes like a cat, and he followed some trail that was known to him but invisible to me.

After more than an hour, I noticed a change in the forest around us. The undergrowth drew back from us and gave way to towering oak trees surrounded by patches of soft grass. I realized I could see fairly well, and I wondered if the dawn had crept up on us.

Django stopped me, and pointed to a swell in the earth to our left. A halo of light shone beyond, and I could smell sweet smoke.

Django whispered. "It is as I feared. Your friend was captured by the old ones, the Druids."

"Why? I thought Druids were in England, anyway."

"Theirs is an ancient belief, and it covers all of Europe. It is late May so these are not ritual bale-fires that burn, we may bless our Lord for that." Django looked at me with concern. "They may have been drawn by the spell over your friend Poe. It is like contagion in their forests, and so they seek to cure it."

I brightened. "You think they might help him then."

"Hardly. The only way an enchantment breaks is with the death of the enchanter"—his look was grim—"or the enchanted."

We crawled together up the slope, and looked over the top to the grove below. Men dressed in full length, grey robes moved busily about. Two men stood watching the others. They held long sticks with scythes made of gold on the end. Each stick was draped in mistletoe. Fires burned in three large heaps which made the points of a triangle. Within this boundary hung two wicker baskets suspended from A-frames.

In one a man shouted angrily at the Druids as he pulled helplessly at the wicker bars. In the other Broccoli lay crumpled like a broken toy. Piles of dry wood and kindling were heaped beneath each basket.

I grabbed Django's arm, and whispered. "Does that mean what I think it means?"

"I believe they mean to burn them, yes."

"For crying out loud, there must be twenty guys down there. What will we do?"

Django pointed away from the east-most fire to the side of the grove. Our ponies were there, as was a large black stallion. Near them were piles of clothing, and weapons.

"If you can get down there, then perhaps you can find that man's weapons. Take them, and I will create a diversion on the opposite side. As soon as I have their attention, get to the center and free the man and Broccoli. But whatever you do, free the man first."

"Why?"

"He will make an ally, and at these odds, we need all the allies we can get."

Django took my hand. "You will do well, young man. If I do not make it, take your friend onward there," he pointed northeast. "Continue to the Jura Mountains. It's about a week away. You will come to the village of Ain. Find the blacksmith; his name is Germond. He will take you to the Pass of the Lamb. It is the only safe way to the Valley of the Baron."

"Be careful, Django."

He grinned. "Careful people don't take on lunatics in the forest. Be fast, little man." He crept away, and I was alone. There was nothing for me to do, but get after it.

I slipped from tree to tree working my way down to the animals. From the slope these men had looked like mystical priests, but at closer range I saw them for what they were, raggedy men with stringy hair and harsh, bright lights of madness in their eyes. It made it worse

40

to know they were human, and fear ran through me in cold waves that made me shiver.

I tried to slip up on the cache of weapons unseen. When at last I was in reaching distance, I saw most of the weapons were crude things, lengths of iron bar and a few, poor swords. But among them was a sword of far better quality. It rested in a scabbard scored with lines of silver.

I was sure it had been taken from the man in the basket. I reached in and grabbed it, and pulled it to me where I lay out of sight behind a tree. Behind me the ponies continued to crop the grass as if nothing were happening. The men in the grove had not seen me. I reached in again, with the sword tip this time, and searched clumsily for Broccoli's things. There was no sign of his belt or talisman. I found his sword but it lay pinned beneath other weapons, and I feared I could not take it quietly. I left it there.

I drew back from the pile and sat with my back to the tree, thinking. Something Django said rang a bell with me, and I was beginning to get an idea. If only I was right and Broccoli still had his belt. I turned to look out again. The men continued with their rituals, whatever they were. Where the heck was Django?

As if in answer there was a scream from the far side of the camp. A man came running in, blood flowing from his shoulder. The others raced toward him and began to shout as they swept into the woods.

I didn't stop to worry if all were gone or not. I ran to the baskets in the center of the grove. I ignored the shouting around me as I shoved the sword through the wicker bars to the man inside.

"Free yourself," I shouted, then sped to the other basket before he could answer.

"Broccoli, Broccoli, can you hear me?" Broccoli's basket was silent. I leaped up and grabbed hold of the bars. I pulled myself hand over hand until I could work my arm inside. I hung suspended in a whirl of noise and confusion. Broccoli lay cold and still within the wicker prison. His face had gone blue-black from the venom racing inside his veins.

The roar grew louder around me and I heard the sounds of curses and fighting. I knew the diversion was over and that I had only seconds to act. Had Broccoli changed the settings on his belt since he'd tried to show it to me before? Was he even wearing it? Desperately I hung from one hand as I groped for the time belt.

Hands clutched at my feet as I touched it, at last. Without thinking I kicked at the hands and they let go. I fumbled for the belt again.

"Burn them!" someone shouted, and torches were thrown into the heap of wood below us. A tremendous blast of heat struck me as I grabbed frantically for the belt. Something on the belt felt like it might be a button, so I pushed it. Broccoli was beginning to stir, weakly. Flames roared up around me, and I yelled with pain and frustration as I let go. I pushed off with my feet and fell away from the pyre to the cool earth below.

Rough hands grabbed me, pulled me to my feet, but my eyes searched for the basket. An ear splitting cry tore the night air.

"Winstooooon!" My tears ran as flames engulfed the basket.

It hadn't worked.

8

So close! I'd been so close! Now the basket was like a balloon of fire. Nothing could live within that inferno. Broccoli was gone, and I was stuck here in the past forever.

The hands which held me twisted me around. Across from me Django and the prisoner I'd given the sword to were surrounded. Django's side was stained with blood, whether his own or another's I could not tell. He and the tall stranger stood back to back like mismatched bookends, holding the Druids at bay.

One of the two men who held the sickles strode across the grove to my side. As he neared I saw him more clearly. He was stooped with age. He grabbed my shoulder with his gnarled hand and squeezed it hard enough to hurt. The man who'd held me before released me as the priest dragged me toward the others.

"Halt. Surrender your arms, or I will destroy the child."

44

Django looked unsure, and the thought of that noble soldier surrendering because of me was more than I could bear. I let my anger carry me. I turned and grabbed the hand on my shoulder. I sank my teeth deep into the priest's hand. He howled like a monkey and I grunted with satisfaction as I felt flesh rip beneath my teeth.

I spun from his grasp shouting, "Take that, you dweeb!"

The priest held his hand, and stared at me with a puzzled frown. "Dweeb? What is a dweeb?"

It was ridiculous. Here I was in an ancient grove surrounded by tree worshippers and haunted rabbits and guys with swords and my neighbor burning up in a basket and this priest fool decides he wants to know what a dweeb is. I suddenly realized I didn't know.

"It is a word of power. Beware, fools! You trifle with a monk from Prester John!" Django sang out. He glared at me as if trying to tell me something. Then I got it. Dweeb didn't translate because I had no clear definition for it myself. So it had no meaning for these guys. Django wanted to run a scam, maybe scare them into letting us go.

I thought about trying some cuss words, but no, they probably had words for those. The druids were nervous, but it wouldn't last. Superstitious they may be, but dweeb would only take us so far, powerful as it may have been. What else wouldn't translate? I looked down at my shoes and found the answer.

"That's right, doofus. You nerds have really gone too far. Don't make me Reebok you guys."

"Reebok?"

"That's right." I spun at a druid who was sneaking up behind me. "Kodak!" I shouted, and he leaped back as if stung. I turned again to the priest, threw my arms wide and began the biggest bluff of my life.

"O mighty Motorola, strike these Sony fools with Toyota and smite their . . . their Kleenex with Robitussin." Spinning like a dervish I worked my way closer to Django and the stranger as I chanted. "Kellogg's, Listerine, Levi's, Polaroid, Nintendo. Sega, Yamaha, and Mattel." I reached Django's side. I stopped and pulled the dagger Nen had given me. I pointed it at the priest who paled in the firelight. "CNN to you, you Tonka." I waved furiously as I worked my way up to the big ones, the megacorporations.

"Purina, Nabisco, Proctor and Gamble, General Electric and"—my dagger pointed directly at the burning basket as I hollered—"Coca-Cola!"

The Druids gasped. Some fell to their knees and cried out. A dull hiss filled the air, and I gaped with surprise as huge clouds of yellow gas erupted around the basket. Everyone was backing away from us now. Even Django was looking about nervously.

46

The stranger watched with interest, then said, "That Coca-Cola seemed to be particularly effective."

With a tearing sound the basket fell from its frame and the fire below went out before the onslaught of gas. From the woodpile stepped a figure with hideous bug eyes, and tendrils trailing from its head. It was dressed in a shimmering suit of foil. It held a box before it.

"What is it, Winston?"

"Beats the heck out of me."

The creature lifted a finger in the air, then pressed down on the box. Immediately a wall of sound blared across the grove. Druids were scattering in every direction, wailing as they fled into the woods. I grinned as I noticed Django and the stranger cowering before the creature. I patted their shoulders. "Hey man, it's only rock and roll. Get up." Broccoli walked forward and pulled off the gas mask. "Give me five, Poe man!"

"You got it," he said.

We slapped palms and grinned like idiots. Broccoli turned off the boom box, much to the relief of Django and the stranger.

"What was that magic?"

I laughed. "That was 'Jumping Jack Flash,' my man. The one and only Rolling Stones. After all it's the fifteenth century. You gotta go with classic rock."

9

Broccoli and I tied straps around the gas tanks. We added the gas mask, fire suit, and boom box. He'd brought an extra time belt for me as well as the stuff. We watched as the junk vanished, returned to our own time.

"We can't risk leaving modern technology behind," Broccoli said. "It wouldn't do for an archaeologist to find Halon gas canisters and a Sony boom box from the fifteenth century."

"I understand," I said. "Still, I wouldn't mind having a few things to help us, like an Uzi or a bazooka."

"We'll just have to do without." Broccoli stopped and looked at me. "It was a near thing, you know."

"I didn't think it worked. I thought I pushed the wrong button."

"You did. But you got through to me. I came to just long enough to figure out what was happening. The button you pushed changed the time reading. I ended up in Hawaii, around 1700."

"No kidding," I said. "It's lucky it was so far forward. I took the chance that if you could move beyond the time of your enchanter's life, the spell would be broken."

"It did. I began to heal. The natives there were very kind to me. They fed me, and took care of me. I spent almost two weeks there."

"Do any surfing?" I asked.

"Not hardly."

"Too bad. I hate to think of you suffering on a beach while we're having so much fun here getting our throats cut."

"Hey, I got back in time, didn't I? I needed the time to get well."

I sighed. "Yes, I guess you did." We walked across the grove and rejoined Django and the stranger. Django had recovered Broccoli's weapon from the pile. He made no mention of the incredible magic he'd witnessed this evening, and we offered no explanations.

Django gestured toward the stranger. "This is Jacques Bienville. These are the monks, Poe and Winston."

Jacques bowed formally. "I owe you my life. I am at your service."

"How did you come to be captured?" Broccoli asked.

"They descended on me as I slept, and overpowered me with their force of numbers. I had traveled many days, and in my weariness was taken unawares."

"To where do you travel?"

49

"I seek Baron Radoul."

"Indeed," whispered Broccoli. Django's eyes grew wide, and I could see suspicion cross his face. "And this Baron, is he a friend of yours?"

Jacques shook his head. "I do not know him. I have heard he is a great wizard. I have . . . need of such a one."

Broccoli considered for a moment. He looked at me, but I could only shrug. He looked at Django who shook his head. The dwarf did not like it.

"We, too, seek the Baron. Perhaps it would be safer to travel together. Would you join us?"

Jacques bowed again. "If it is your wish. But I do not think your friend agrees."

Django spat. "I have little faith in those who seek to conduct business with the Blood Baron."

"Yet we travel to the Baron ourselves. Let us not judge without facts," said Broccoli. He turned to Bienville. "Your business with the Baron is . . . ?"

"Personal," replied Jacques. His face was hard as stone.

"Let him come," I said.

Broccoli asked, "Why?"

"It is the right thing to do."

"How can you be sure?" asked Django.

"I don't know. But I am." The stranger's face did not change, but as he looked at me I thought I saw gratitude in his eyes. And something more. I felt a great sadness and tragedy coming from the man. I knew I was right. But *how* did I know I was right? It was a little spooky.

"Very well," said Broccoli. "We shall go on together. Django, are you wounded?"

"No," he said. "It's the blood of one of those godless lunatics." He pointed at Bienville. "Hear me now. These two are entrusted to my care by the Maid of Orleans. Betray their faith and I shall wear *your* blood as well."

The man offered an amused smile. "Understood."

"Then let's be off before those moon-loving fools find their manhood and return for us."

We mounted our horses and rode eastward, toward the rising sun.

◢10◣

I suffered from dreams—grim, dark nightmares filled with howling shapes and slavering fangs. The dreams frightened me. The wizard was in all of them; he strode through my nightmares like a god, tall and mighty. Dabble, too, was there, his near human face void of expression, but his eyes shimmering with threat, actually pulsing as if his head were filled with swarming wasps.

I dragged through the days as we rode toward Ain. Broccoli watched me with a worried frown, and tried to help, but I told him nothing. I resented him and his stupid adventure. I missed my home. Even lawn work seemed fun right now. Django tried to make my going easier, but I ignored him too. Only Bienville had sense enough to keep to himself.

Days of travel and nights of terror-filled nightmares left me drained. Two days from the village we camped beside a deserted farm. Broccoli went hunting in the wild fields while I collapsed on my bedroll. I could barely hold my eyes open, but if I closed them, he would be there—the wizard! He would laugh at me, and look into my deepest soul.

That gaze terrified me. I knew the power behind those eyes was greater than anything I might imagine. I feared that what it directed me to do, I would do. I whimpered to myself as I lay on the hard ground.

Broccoli returned with a bag of onions he'd scrounged in the field. With great care he drew a circle around our campsite. I watched as he scratched lines in the earth to form a star inside the circle. He laid an onion at each point of the star, then surrounded me where I lay with a fine line of salt.

"What are you doing?" I asked.

"I think something's happening to you, and I don't think it's natural. Are you having nightmares?"

I shuddered. "Beyond nightmares," I whispered.

"Tell us about them," he said.

I did not answer.

Django and Jacques Bienville sat near us. Both men were careful to sit outside the circle of salt. Jacques looked at his hand, then up at the moon, three-quarters full.

"Sometimes," he said, "it helps to talk."

All was silence for several moments, then slowly I began to tell them.

"There is a hillside, bright in the moonlight, and the hare is there, the one that howls. As it screams, a wolf approaches. It dives at the hare which flops over onto its back. The wolf has it in its jaws, but the hare's hind feet are powerful, its claws razor sharp, and it tears at the belly of the wolf. The wolf gasps and dies as its guts are ripped away.

"The wizard watches and laughs. The hare gets to its feet and nuzzles at the carcass of the wolf. It tears the heart from the wolf and eats it, as the wolf rolls down the hill to my feet. Only now, it is no wolf, but a man!"

Bienville sucks in his breath, and Django eyes him sharply. Broccoli only nods. "Go on," he says.

"Then I'm at this—I don't know, a castle I guess. But more like a house. Dabble is there, dressed like a butler, and everywhere I go he goes with me. The wizard seems to be in every room we go through, working. The things he does . . ." I shivered and pulled my blanket up tight around me. "I can't tell you, it's too horrible, but I help him. *I help him!*"

I looked at them in shame, but they only stared back at me sadly, without judgement. I wanted to scream at them, *Don't you see? It means I will betray you!* Instead I shut my eyes and sobbed. I thought of home, my mom, my pals. Eventually, I fell asleep.

I awoke feeling better than I had for days. I tried to recall dreaming and couldn't. Broccoli looked at me, concern on his face.

"Did you sleep well? Are you better?"

"Yeah, I guess I just got too tired to dream."

"I don't think so," said Broccoli. "I think something was trying to attack you through your dreams through some kind of spell. It was magic, Winston."

"But why?"

"To weaken us further. Everything he's done has been toward that end. The onions and salt shielded you from the attack. That's why you could sleep."

I gave him my most doubtful look. "Onions. And salt. Against magic. No offense, Broccoli, but that's about the lamest thing I've ever heard."

He smiled. "Suit yourself. But don't argue with results. Come on. We're having breakfast."

I rolled my blanket tight, and walked to put it on my horse. As I did, I noticed something like a chunk of coal on the ground. It was an onion, blackened and charred. Slowly, I walked the circle and found all five. Each was blackened like the first. An aroma of sickness came from them.

I walked back to where I'd slept and knelt down. Where the salt had been was a faint line in the dirt. I touched it. The salt and dirt had fused, leaving a slender ring like glass.

I joined the others at the fire.

"How many of those onions do you have left?" I asked.

"About a dozen."

I shook my head. "Not enough. As soon as we eat, let's find some more."

"So, maybe I'm not as stupid as you thought I was, eh?"

"I'm convinced," I said. "Let's see can we find some brussels sprouts, too. If onions slow him down, then brussels sprouts might just kill him outright."

"I don't think it works like that," said Broccoli.

"It never hurts to try," I said. Breakfast tasted better than it had for days.

11

The village of Ain lay at the foothills like a dog at the feet of its master, sleepy, but alert. Should the mountains send snow or thunder, it would find the village ready. But beneath this mood of readiness lay a sadness I could not quite put my finger on. It was Broccoli who named it.

"They are weary," he said.

The village was small, barely a dozen buildings, but it counted the surrounding farmers as townsmen, and so it thrived as best it could so close to the shadow of Baron Radoul.

"He has little to do with us," said Germond, the blacksmith. He had welcomed us with great joy at the sight of Django, and I felt safer than I had felt since leaving my own time. Even the stranger, Bienville, seemed to brighten in the smithy's presence. "He has little to do with us, and we have less to do with him." Germond drank heartily from a bottle of wine, and belched with contentment.

57

Django said, "Then you are fortunate he has yet to cast his eye in your direction."

"Let him cast! By the sacred bones of Saint Steven we will die gladly before we give in to the likes of him!"

"Brave words," murmured Django.

"Why not? I am a brave man. Everyone says so."

I smiled at this gentle giant of a man. His brags were so innocent, given in such good humor, that I could not help but like him.

"Why not come with us?" asked Django innocently.

"Hah! That would be good for you, eh? Why, I'd catch that demon Baron by his scrawny throat and choke the life from him, the child killer!" The smithy's eyes closed as he imagined his tremendous valor. "No worries for you then. You could just stand and watch." He gestured as if encompassing the world.

"But my poor village! The women would cry and waste away to nothing if I were to leave." He shook his head. "And the rascals and fools who make up the men would have their way with everyone, ruining the economy and bringing disgrace on us all. No, I fear my destiny is here, much as I would love to come with you."

The smithy gazed at the fire, as if truly saddened by the burdens his greatness placed upon him. Bienville snickered softly to himself, and Germond rolled a shrewd eye in his direction.

"And you, good sir. What purpose does so obviously fine a gentleman have with a scoundrel like the Baron, eh?"

Bienville was silent. Broccoli said, "Yes, tell us. Perhaps our purposes coincide."

The man regarded Broccoli with his melancholy gaze. "That is unlikely. My reasons are my own, but they are not wicked, I assure you."

"Sometimes one must seek a devil to fight a devil," Broccoli said softly.

Bienville's face grew pale in the firelight. "What do you know?" he said, his voice trembling.

"I know little, Jacques, but I suspect much. Keep your secret if you must, but do not be too sure our interests are so different," said Broccoli.

The man rose. His emotions seemed barely held in check. "You do not know. You could not." His eyes looked at one, then the other of us. Django and Germond were silent. "I know what you are thinking, but I will not betray you."

"Indeed, there's a promise I will help you keep," promised Django. His smile spread in a nasty line across his face.

"Enough!" shouted Germond. "I will not allow the harmony of my fire to be ruined by this bickering among friends." He rose, still clutching his wine bottle, and tottered slowly before Bienville and Django. "Now stop this, or by the holy elbows of St. Paul I will thrash both of you to within an inch of your ungrateful lives!''

"You are right, of course," Bienville said. "We travel too far and through too much danger to travel as anything but friends. I must consider this carefully. Perhaps I should go on ahead." He rose and headed for the door. "Good night, to all. I will sleep on it, and tell you my decision in the morning." With that he left.

Django sighed. "Here's hoping he goes on alone. I do not trust him."

"Here's hoping he does not," said Broccoli. "I think he is the reason we are here."

I stared in shock at Broccoli. Could it be true? Was Bienville the Amber Man?

12

The next morning Django, Broccoli, and I told Bienville everything. He listened calmly to our story, but it was impossible to tell how much he believed. We waited for him to say something. At last he looked at Broccoli.

"Of course, I knew there was something extraordinary when you stepped from the fire. This"—he stopped, waving his hand in the air above him—"this story about the future is rather hard to believe. And as for me being a werewolf . . ."

"Do you deny it?" asked Broccoli.

"What does it matter? You are convinced." Bienville studied our faces for a moment. "If I am, I do not understand how my turning away now will help me."

"But don't you see," I said. "The Baron will betray you. He is going to trap you in amber for the next five hundred years! And you will not die. In our time you will awake and the curse will be upon the earth again. If you turn away now that will never happen. Broccoli and I can go home to our own time. Everything will be all right.''

"Except for some poor soul cursed by the moon," Jacques said angrily. "He will carry on in torment until at last he finds a way to take his own life that he may find hell that much more quickly!'' He turned to Broccoli. "Or perhaps, young wizard, you carry a cure for this curse in your pack."

Broccoli looked away. "I know of no cure."

"I thought not." Jacques stood, and grabbed his things. "I ride on to the Baron. Do as you please, but I ride on." He smiled. "I think you will come, too. After all, you've just told me it is what you are here to do. Perhaps you are the tools of change for me.'' The stranger's eyes were flat. I could not guess what he was thinking. "Besides, I may not be your precious were-wolf after all. Dare you risk it?"

With that he opened the door and stepped outside. I threw a miserable look at Broccoli. "What a jerk," I said.

Broccoli's eyes gazed off as if to some far land. "I'm not so sure. Perhaps we have been hasty. Django, how many days until the full moon?"

"Four," said the dwarf.

"And how many days until we arrive at the Baron's stronghold?"

There was silence, then Django said, "Five."

Broccoli sighed. "So, one way or another we will

know soon enough, eh?'' Broccoli reached over and patted my shoulder. ''I'm sorry, Winston. I know you want to go home.''

I felt all the frustration, fear, and anger rising in me. I shrugged away from his hand. ''So send me. You have another belt.''

Broccoli spread his hands. ''You know what the spirits have said. For some reason you are critical to this. I cannot do it without you. Please, Winston.''

I stood. My mind was made up. ''I'm not going to do it. I've had enough,'' my voice trembled. ''I'm fed up with magic, and madmen, and eating lousy food, and sleeping on the ground. I'm tired of feeling guilty for wanting to be safe at home. I never asked for any of this. Now, let me go home.''

Broccoli looked at Django, then up at me. The soldier said quietly, ''He has done much for one so young. His bravery is without question. But you cannot force a man to your quest. I am with you, but not unless you heed young Winston's wishes. I was there at the Druid fire. He has nothing to prove to me.''

I could have kissed him. ''Thank you,'' I whispered, but he only stared at me, his face impassive.

Broccoli reached in his bag. He pulled out the extra belt and stood. ''Come here,'' he said. I stood with my arms stretched out as he strapped it around me and set the controls. He stepped back, and I lowered my arms.

He put his hands on my shoulders and looked at me

from his pudgy face. "I cannot help what I am. Sometimes destiny touches us, and makes us move in ways we cannot account for. Despite my few years, I cannot truthfully say I have ever been young. I have never had a friend other than the spirits who speak in my head. I don't know what it is to be homesick; my parents are always away, working. Home is kind of an empty place for me."

"I'm sorry," I said. I'd never thought how terribly sad it must be to be like Broccoli. I felt worse than ever about leaving him.

"I'd like to think we could have been friends," he said.

I smiled. "We *are* friends." I hugged him and slapped his back. "Good luck. I'll never forget this."

"Nor I you," he said and pushed the button. The scene vanished.

13

Broccoli pushed the button and I fell, screaming through time. I plummeted for what seemed like days until I landed with a hard thud on soft earth. The wind was knocked from me and I struggled to regain my breath. When it came I was sickened by the stench of the putrid earth in which I lay.

I raised my head, gasping for purer air, and struggled to my feet. Night hung over me like a pall, and I cried out when the moon revealed my landing site for what it was: a graveyard!

I twirled slowly like a stupid drunkard taking in the sights around me, the naked stones, the trees clawing at the night sky, the yellow moon, pale against the velvet dark.

I heard a noise and twisted my head in time to see earth crack as a dark, scaly hand broke through the reeking soil to reach for me. I ran from the cemetery as other evils lurched from the ground, their backs bent, their eyes hot with hate and fury in their rotted skulls, their arms held out as if to take me.

I came to a fence and hurdled it. My shoe caught the top and I tumbled down a wet slope. I rolled all the long way down, until at last I was dumped, gasping, into a frigid creek. The icy water swept me away, tossed me from bank to bank, never close enough to grab for safety, as if it were alive this one time to torment this one boy.

The water calmed and I floated, dazed, through a gauntlet of grasping oaks, their limbs dripping with slime. The creek rounded a bend, and there before me stood the hanging trees. Django hung from the limbs like an obscene Christmas bulb, his face purple, his tongue swollen. Flies as large as beetles crawled across his poor body. I cried in horror and shame as I floated past.

"I'm sorry, sorry," I tried to shout, but he could not hear me. Another bend, and I could hear the shrieks before I got there. Broccoli hung from a tree, struggling as a creature—not quite man, not quite wolf—held him by the waist. The monster roared as it saw me, and its eyes burned like embers. It opened its mouth wide; its teeth gleamed like knives in the moonlight. Its head ducked toward Broccoli's belly. And the sound it made . . .

"No!" I screamed at the top of my voice. "No! No! No! No!"

"Winston, it's okay. You're all right." Caring arms held me and I collapsed, sobbing into my father's chest.

"I've killed them," I whimpered. "I've killed them all."

"No, Winston," Dad whispered. I straightened up, and wiped my eyes. Behind Dad I could see Mom standing in the doorway looking worried. Dad ran his fingers through my hair, pulling it from my forehead and brushing it back.

"It was just a dream. Who did you think you killed?"

"Nobody," I said quietly. "I—I can't remember. It was so strong, and now—it's gone."

Dad gave me a doubtful look. Mom came and sat beside him on the edge of my bed.

"Winston, this has been going on for over two weeks. Don't you think you should tell us what's bothering you?" she asked, her voice soft with concern. She put her hand to my face. "You've never had nightmares before."

"It's all those stupid horror movies," said Dad. "I knew they'd get to him one of these days."

Mom continued to look at me. I avoided her stare. She did not look convinced. "Is it the Amber Man? Don't be ashamed. Mona Davis told me her kids are having nightmares too since—since *it* happened."

"Irresponsible reporting is what it is," said Dad, rising. "It's not like kids don't have enough *real* things

67

to worry about in this world; they don't need the media feeding their fantasies with imaginary monsters.''

"We don't know what happened over there, John. No one does.''

"Terrorists. I'll bet you anything. They broke into those labs, killed everybody, and stole the Amber Man.''

Mom looked at Dad as if he were a little kid. "Now why would they do that?''

"Who knows why they do anything? All I know is, it's a lot more reasonable than thinking some guy from the fifteenth century awoke and ripped the throats out of a bunch of scientists.''

"John! You're just making it worse!'' Mom cuddled me into her arms, and gave Dad her best watch-out look. Dad looked ashamed of himself.

"Hey, sport, I'm sorry,'' he said. "I'm just worried about you is all. It comes out funny sometimes.''

"I know,'' I said. I pulled away from Mom. "It's all right. Really. I just need to go to sleep.'' I lay back down and closed my eyes.

Mom and Dad fussed around me a little bit more, gave up finally, and went away. They kept my door open a crack so they could hear me better. I turned over and looked out the window toward the Poe house.

Where were Broccoli's parents? I hadn't seen them since I'd come back more than two weeks before. Every day I expected Broccoli or someone to show up, and no one did. I turned my eyes.

Spider-Man stared out at me from a Marvel Comics poster on my wall. "What are you looking at?" I muttered. Sure, it's easy to accuse someone else when you're a super-hero. "So what would you do, hotshot?"

Spider-Man stayed silent, but he didn't have to speak. I *knew* what he'd do. Go back and kick some wizard butt, *that's* what he'd do.

I snuck from my bed to the chest of drawers and opened the bottom one. I kept a small, leather bag there along with my full-wrist slingshot. I opened the drawstring and dropped three perfect silver balls into my palm. Each was about the size of a marble. I'd melted them down from some of Mom's silver from the attic the day the news broke about the Amber Man. They felt cool and full of purpose in my palm. I clenched my fist and raised it to my cheek. My hand throbbed.

"Why me?" I asked of no one. No one answered.

I returned the silver to my pouch, and dressed quickly. I dug in the back of my closet and recovered the dagger Nen had given me, well hidden since my return home. I dropped the silver in my pocket and stuffed the slingshot in a special holster made for it. I tied the holster to my leg.

As quietly as a ghost I slipped through the window to my roof, and dropped from there to the ground. The back door of Poe's house was still open. I crept inside and moved through the cluttered rooms toward the time

69

cabinet. I recovered my talisman and time belt from the spirit table where I'd left them.

At the cabinet it hit me I had no idea how to work it or where to go. I backed up and thought for a minute. I returned to the spirit table and sat down. Palms flat on the table top I called for help.

"Sacajawea, if you can hear me I need your help. It was wrong to leave them, and I must repair the damage I've done. Please help me, gentle spirit. Please."

There was silence for almost five minutes. I continued to concentrate, and kept pleading over and over for her help. At last, just as I was ready to give up, there came an odor like pine needles, and deep forest. The cabinet began to hum.

I felt my stomach grow tight as I realized what I was about to do. "God help me," I whispered. The numbers on the cabinet came to a stop and I stepped through.

There was that now familiar tingle as I zipped through time, then I found myself high on a cliff looking down. Below me lay a wasteland, a valley made dry and sick through neglect and pollution. At the center of this sickness stood the château of the wizard: Baron Radoul!

Around the castle dim figures could be seen moving in a shuffling, eerie watch. Lakes of mist and fog moved slowly across the scarred earth alternately hiding and revealing the gloomy castle.

It occurred to me that I never had learned to operate the time belt properly. If Sacajawea had messed up, if

70

Broccoli was already dead I might be stuck in this time forever. I sighed. It was too late to worry about that now.

The fear was worse than it had been in my dream. Somehow, the sight of that castle unnerved me more than the memory of my nightmare. I gritted my teeth and started the treacherous climb down the cliff.

⌃14⌄

It took almost an hour to reach the bottom. The rocks were slick from mist, and more than once I lost my footing to find myself dangling in terror above the rocks below. Nevertheless, I took the time to gather good hard stones for my slingshot whenever I came across them. The silver must be saved, and while I had a dagger, I had little confidence in my ability—or willingness—to use it. But with a slingshot I could hurt them. I was the best shot in town, and knew it.

At last the cliffside began to slope gently, and the last few feet were an easy slide. I came to a stop and sat waiting, listening. I was alone and in no mood to be captured right off the bat. My heroics would look pretty silly if some ditzy guard put an arrow through my heart before I even found out what happened to my friends.

The night was quiet, no sounds of animals in the bushes, no cries of night-birds in the distance. Above me a cloud of fog drifted in like a huge buffalo to scratch its back against the cliff. I thanked my lucky stars it had waited for me to finish my climb. In that dense mist I'd have been blinded.

Despite the valley's look of devastation from above it was actually not unpleasant at the valley floor. New growth still struggled to make its way against the older, dead landscape of twisted trees and battered stone. The air smelled slightly of recent rain, with just a touch of peaches or some other, sweet, familiar scent too faint to identify as anything else.

I checked my small store of armaments and set off. Softly, I crept from tree to tree, bush to bush making a zig-zag course across the valley. Somewhere ahead I would encounter others, but it was impossible to gauge distance in these conditions. The castle could be miles away or just ahead for all I knew.

I was startled by a sudden glimpse of the moon as it slipped like a silver dollar from the palm of one cloud to another. Remembering the wolf it made me shudder. How many days had it been full? Four days to the full moon, Django had said; five days to the château. Could I be ahead of them?

I became aware of the first faint mutter of voices and stopped to listen. The words were unintelligible, mere shades of words from this distance, but I grew more cautious. I had no way to judge how sound might travel over such open ground. My approach grew ever slower and more cautious as the sound of voices gained volume.

When at last I could see them it was all I could do to keep myself from turning and running. They were not people at all, but strange constructs of man and beast intermingled: goats with the heads of children, bleating with mindless cravings; a man with the head and hindquarters of a bear; a woman with a dog's tail, and legs to go with it.

There were dozens of these things all jabbering from time to time, none of them making sense. Some huddled around a large fire, while others wandered away and returned without purpose. And all of them watched the fire through eyes grown bright with madness. It made me want to be sick, but I held it back. I had to get around them.

I backtracked carefully, then swung wide to the left, wide enough—I hoped—that none of their several wanderers would come across me by accident. My need for speed was no match for the need for stealth. Terror had been with me for so long that I was growing dull to it. What I had to do, I would do. I moved on.

Soon I heard muttering from another direction. I followed it warily. Pieces of the castle jutted stone-shouldered through the fog and then vanished again, and I realized I was closer than I thought. Meanwhile, the new voices rose gleefully, as if in anticipation of some great event. I took two steps, then froze as I heard a rushing sound behind me.

Without thinking I leaped into a tree to my right and began to climb swiftly. The rushing sound had been the man-beasts running toward the new voices. They had not noticed me. From my new vantage I could see light some hundred feet away. A small rise in the ground had hidden a slope which led to the castle grounds below.

I climbed higher. The tree was perfect for climbing. I thought of the goats with children's faces and wondered how many of those poor tortured children had once climbed this tree as I did now. For the first time I realized I was angry. I swore that the Baron would pay for the horror he'd inflicted on those children, if for nothing else.

From the top of the tree I could see a crowd of the man-things cheering hoarsely as a wagon rolled slowly from the castle. No horses pulled this wagon, it simply rolled as if by magic. I gasped at the sight of the wolf-man in the wagon. He looked different than he had in my dream. I could barely recognize the man, Bienville, in this new shape. It stood tall, like a man, in the wagon bed. It spread its arms and howled before the crowd which cringed before the wolf's power.

The wolf-man bent over and plucked a small figure from the wagon floor. It's wolf-cry changed to words as it shouted, "Meat!"

Here was a word with meaning for the man-things

75

who yelled, "Meat! Meat!" in frantic, slavering response. And all the while Django hung struggling like a cat at the end of the wolf-man's arm.

There was no time to think. I grabbed my slingshot, and fumbled out the first shooter in the bag. It was only a rock, but it would have to do. I aimed as I have never aimed before and sent the stone whistling through the air. It struck the wolf-man dead in the temple.

The wolf-man's howl split the night, and the man-things shouted in fear and confusion. Django fell with the werewolf into the wagon bed, but was up in an instant, tugging at the wolf-man's shoulders hollering, "Meat! Meat!" as he tumbled the werewolf from the wagon.

The crowd of things grew silent, as they looked in confusion at the beast that brought the meat now turned to meat itself.

"Meat! Meat! Don't you understand, you imbeciles, meat!"

A large creature with the head and horns of a bull stepped forward and sniffed cautiously at the wolf-man. "Meat?" it asked, making sure.

"Yes, you bull-brained, butt-head! Now eat him before he comes to and kills me! Meat!"

"Meat!" shouted the bull-man joyously. That was good enough for the rest of them. "Meat!" they all shrieked and the lot of them fell upon the wolf-man like ravenous dogs, which—I suppose—technically some of them were.

I was out of the tree in an instant and joined Django as he raced toward the castle. Behind us sounds of joy and hunger slowly gave way to cries of rage and struggle.

"Old wolfie's come to," said Django grimly. "Let us hope they keep him busy for at least another minute."

"Wolfie?" I said, despite myself.

"We've become very close, he and I," said Django by way of explanation.

Loud screams came from the melee behind us as we reached the wall.

"What now?" I panted.

Django pulled at a board beneath the wall, and uncovered a hole.

"Where does this go?" I asked.

"No time," he growled and pushed me through the hole. I went tumbling like a stone through the darkness.

⒂

I landed hard on my side, and immediately began to roll downward. Perhaps fifteen feet further on I came to a stop, the breath knocked out of me, and my left arm throbbing from the landing. Moments later Django slid to a stop beside me, and helped me sit up.

When I got my bearings I looked up and saw the wolf-man snarling and ranting at the hole above.

"Don't worry," said Django. "He can't get through. Sometimes there are advantages to being small, eh?" I nodded weakly, and felt my arm. I'd bruised it pretty well, but I could still use it all right. Nothing was broken or sprained.

Django helped me up.

"Let's get ourselves lost before someone gets smart about where we are."

I followed him down a black corridor. It was a tight squeeze even for us. We walked stooped over in the blackness. I had no sense of direction. Eventually we came to a stop, and Django produced a torch which he lit.

We'd come to a small chamber, about the size of a bathroom. Django fixed the torch in the wall and sat across from me. He pointed to the slingshot in its holster.

"What is that?"

"A weapon," I said.

"Good, we can use all the weapons we can get. I lost mine when they captured us."

"Here," I said, and gave him Nen's dagger. "It's of no use to me."

"I will borrow it for a while," he said. He hefted the blade appraisingly. "Now that I am free, I can get better weapons. In the days when I was Hop-frog I took the opportunity to hide things against the day when I might need them. I left a store or two of things cached in case I should ever return."

"What happened?" I asked. "Where is Broccoli? Was that Bienville back there?"

Django's face grew somber. "Aye, that was him, the poor fool. But there is more to that story than there seems."

"Is Broccoli alive?"

"So far." Django threw the blade into the earth at his feet. He wiped his face, and I realized how incredibly weary he must be.

"If you need to rest awhile—" I started to say.

79

He grunted. "It's best if I tell it now, as it happened. After you left, Germond led us to the Pass of the Lamb. It cuts deep through the Juras to this hidden valley, Radoul's domain. Germond left us there, and we traveled on alone.

"As the full moon neared, Bienville grew increasingly distressed. Broccoli was confused. He told me that he didn't think Bienville had lied about not being a werewolf. Yet, the moon frightened him desperately. One day before its change, Bienville vanished."

Django scowled. "It was supposed to be his watch. Instead, he slipped away and left us. Anyone could have taken us then. And they did.

"We awoke surrounded by a squad of the Baron's pets led by that Dabble creature."

"You mean those man-things?"

"Aye, the Baron has a passion for playing with God's creations. Some of his experiments are nastier than others."

"Those I saw in the valley, they're the failures, aren't they?"

"Yes. The ones with weak minds, and bodies that don't work well wander the valley until they starve to death or kill each other. From time to time he feeds them."

"Meat," I whispered.

"Meat, indeed. I have not thanked you yet for that."

I waved a hand. "Forget it. It's second nature to us Rambo-types. What happened then?"

"They took our things, including Broccoli's belt. They shackled us, and marched us to the château. In the end, Bienville tried to save us, but he was stopped by the orb."

"The orb? What orb?"

"The Protean Orb. It is the tool the Baron uses to wreak change in living things. It also amplifies his other powers. Bienville came as the wolf to try and free us. He killed many of them, but Dabble had the orb, and the Baron reached out from his lair to ensnare the wolf. Now Bienville is completely in his power."

"But I thought you said Broccoli thought Bienville told the truth, that he wasn't a werewolf."

"He is not. He is a *were-man!* The wolf is his natural form. His curse is to walk as a man except during the full moon. And even then he cannot be a true wolf, but must prowl as that beast you saw above."

"So we had it backward!" I was stunned. Well, why couldn't there be a were-man? Maybe all werewolves are actually were-men, and it's only through our own arrogance as humans that we think it otherwise.

My mind reeled at the thought of all this magic. "I don't understand. If the orb is so powerful, why hasn't he taken over the world? And those things he's made, they're all so tragic and useless."

Django nodded. "You're beginning to understand.

81

The Baron's power over the orb is imperfect. He controls less than a hundredth of its power. That's why he needs Broccoli. Apparently your friend is some kind of key to its power."

I gasped, remembering the seance. "Of course! Broccoli is the Key. The spirits told us that. But if Radoul knows that then all of this, the Amber Man, Sacajawea . . ."

". . . was just a trap," Django finished for me. "The Baron was after Broccoli all along!"

⁘16⁙

"**D**oesn't the Baron know these passages are here?"
I asked, following Django through the twisting maze
of corridors.

"He knows. But there are too many to patrol, and his
arrogance is such that he does not care. I am only the Hop-
frog, after all. What is there to fear from the likes of me?"

From what I'd seen of Django, there was plenty to
fear. The wizard's arrogance was a plus as far as I was
concerned. So long as we could wander at will at least
we had a chance, small though it may be.

The passages were no more than hollow trails within
the castle walls. Django continued to call the place a
château, but it was certainly a castle to me. We crept
by endless numbers of rooms, most of them dark and
dead from disuse.

"There is little in this wing," whispered Django.
"The Baron spends most of his time at the far end,
away from the valley."

"Where is he keeping Broccoli?"

"Who knows? We'll try the dungeons first. They are on the way, and perhaps we'll get lucky, but I doubt he's there."

Dungeons. Well, it wasn't much of a surprise. A man who ran around calling himself the Blood Baron and playing mad wizard was certainly the type to have a few dungeons here and there.

"What, no torture chamber?" I muttered.

Django shrugged. "Why bother? All life under the Baron is torture."

"Point taken."

We came to a large chamber, round and high. Shadows danced in the light of Django's torch. He grunted with satisfaction as he lit more torches fitted in the walls. There were boxes jumbled against the walls, a large table in the center of the chamber, and piles of odd junk collected over some long period of time.

Django plundered a large trunk and smiled with satisfaction as he came up with a proper broadsword. He belted the sword to his waist and then hefted an axe with his thick, right arm. He took another dagger, and returned Nen's dagger to me.

"Now we shall see how the Hop-frog bites!" he said.

"Django," I said, touching his shoulder. "Something doesn't make sense. Back at the camp Dabble was going to kill Broccoli. I saw him. Why would he do that if the Baron *wanted* Broccoli to come here? And the bite

84

he received would surely have killed him before we ever arrived.''

Django eyed me thoughtfully. ''You are sure he meant to kill him?''

''The blade was at his throat!''

Django sat on the floor and pursed his lips in thought. ''He might have survived the bite, you know.''

''Perhaps, but he would never have survived the knife. There's another player in this game, Django.''

''Perhaps the wizard from your dream. But I think this Dabble is not so much the wizard's creature as the wizard thinks.'' Django shook his head. ''Wheels within wheels. But something has changed, you see. Dabble could have killed us when he took us in the valley. He did not. What changed between the camp and our capture?''

I felt a chill crawl up my spine. I swallowed hard. ''I changed,'' I whispered. ''I wasn't there!'' I began to pace back and forth as I tried to work it out. ''The spirits made it clear that Broccoli and I are some kind of team. He is the Key, and I am the Chronicler. Perhaps he cannot function as the Key without me.''

Django said excitedly, ''Which means, if Dabble is against the Baron's success, that while you were together the wizard would succeed. And so he sought Broccoli's death. Once apart, the wizard cannot succeed, and Dabble no longer cares if he lives or dies.''

I stopped and stared at Django. ''And that means that

by returning I have doomed us all! Either the Baron will succeed and history will be forever changed by this madman . . .''

". . . or Dabble will kill Broccoli . . .''

". . . leaving me stranded in the past with a *very* disappointed wizard.'' I slumped to the floor, tears stinging my eyes. "It's hopeless.'' But at the same time I was saying that, my brain continued to churn. Something in the back of my mind insisted that I hadn't *quite* worked it all out yet. If I was wrong, there might yet be a way.

Django knew nothing of my thinking. He'd only heard me say it was hopeless. He rose and stood before me, his voice was harsh.

"Is this what they teach the people of your time? To analyze until you can sit content with failure? How wonderful for you. Now, no matter what happens you need not blame yourself. You are convinced whatever you do is wrong, so now you need do nothing. How convenient.''

I jutted my chin and snapped, "That's not fair.''

"Isn't it? The Baron is evil's tool, as is Dabble. That much is plain. Would you, in your despair, be evil's tool as well?

"We, too, have an unseen ally. No man who fights for a righteous cause is ever alone. No man who strives against evil can fail, for to strive means there is hope. But if we do not fight, then we believe the power of darkness is greater than the power of light. Then and only then will evil claim its victory, for then we have forsaken our faith and the devil will rule the earth!''

He stretched his hand to me. ''Well? Do you fight?''

I sighed, and took his hand. He lifted me. ''I fight. Anything to shut you up. You're worse than those television preachers.''

Django grinned. ''Come on. Let's search the dungeons.''

17

The corridor grew ever tighter as we approached the dungeons. A reek of human stench grew stronger as we moved, and my stomach quivered with nausea. We stopped before a stone with a handle, and Django motioned for me to take hold.

Together we strained against the stone. My meager strength could not compare to Django's, but it took the both of us to start it moving. Cords stood out on the dwarf's thick forearms as he strained to pull the stone around behind us.

The smell made me gag as we dropped out of our tunnel and into the dungeon proper. To our right a line of cells carved into the rock stretched beside a narrow trail which dropped away to a stinking, subterranean pool on the left. I peered into its inky depths and shivered at what might lie below its surface.

Django cried out in horror as he looked into the cells. I will never forget the madness of that moment. The cells were packed with the bodies of dozens of the poor, deformed creatures of the Baron's mad imagination. They'd been left to die, alone in the darkness without food or water.

"Even for him, this is too much," said Django as he made the sign of the cross.

"How can so much evil be?" I whispered. The bodies lay, decaying, covered with millions of swarming maggots. Cell bars were covered with slime where many, driven desperate at the end, had beaten out their brains in the attempt to get away.

I tugged at Django's arm. "Go. We . . . we have to go. Please."

"All right," he said. We turned to go back to our tunnel, and Dabble sprang out of the earth before us.

His fingers remained in the hard, claw-like pike shapes he used for burrowing. He swung with blinding speed at Django who barely escaped being cut in half. Django lay before me with Dabble beyond him.

As Django rose and drew his sword Dabble regarded the cells to his right.

"Does it like its sleeping friends?
Soon to join them, Dabble sends."

Django sprang forward with a cry, his sword slicing through the air. Dabble blocked it with his left and the sword chunked as it bit into the arm. Dabble never

89

blinked, but twisted as he drove the other arm for Django's belly.

A thin red line showed where Dabble's fingers had sliced Django. Another inch and the fight would be over. The dwarf's sword still bit into Dabble's arm. Django put a foot against the thing's shoulder, and jerked the blade free.

Dabble fell to the ground, rolled backward then came to his feet, his teeth glinting in the darkness. Django pulled the axe from his belt, and stood spraddle-leg, sword in his left, axe in his right.

He shouted, "Run, Winston. Run while there's still time!"

I whirled and started up the path. There was a grunt of impact behind me, and I turned again. Django moved like a windmill beating desperately at the spitting fiend. For every blow struck by Django, Dabble answered with three, driving the soldier back and back along the path.

"No!" I screamed. "There will be no more death because of me!" I grabbed at the pouch at my waist and dumped the contents on the path. I pulled the sling-shot, and sorted through my ammo. I took one of my three precious balls of silver, and fitted it to the sling.

Trembling with fear, I sighted for Dabble and let fly. The silver spanged off rock to Dabble's right. He laughed with glee as he swung viciously at Django's head.

"At Dabble's feet the dwarf will lie;
Then it's Winston's turn to die!"

I grabbed the second silver shot and aimed again.
Again it whizzed by the creature, even as Dabble deliv-
ered a blow to Django's head. The dwarf fell in a heap
to the ground and Dabble grinned at me as he pointed
at the dwarf with his hideous hand. His arm raised to
strike the final blow even as I sent my last silver bullet
streaking for Dabble's heart.

The ball went through Dabble like a laser beam, leaving a hole I could actually see through. He stood poised,
looking almost human as his hands changed back to
normal. He poked at the hole.

He opened his mouth as if to speak, and the head
of the axe crashed into him as Django struck with all
his might.

The axe landed flat, but the force of the blow was
enough to knock Dabble backward, into the dark pool
behind him. I shuddered with relief that Django was
still alive.

I ran to his side. He was covered in blood, but his
eyes were still bright with spirit.

"Are you okay?"

"I'll live. You should have run."

"And you. Would you have run?"

Django smiled. "This is twice you have saved me. It
does little for my reputation as a fighting man."

I helped him up. I'd been so concerned with Django, I'd forgotten Dabble. The creature struggled in the water like a baby. His face showed no emotion, there was no pleading in the eyes, but it was apparent he could not swim.

The struggles stopped as he slipped beneath the surface.

Before I could even think I dove into the pool after Dabble.

"No, you fool!" Django shouted as I hit the water. It was like swimming through sewage, but I held my breath and swam down until I could grab the creature's hand. It held on without struggle as I swam to the top. I pulled him to the shore and dragged him up.

Django stared at me as if I were crazy, and perhaps I was. He held the axe ready, but Dabble made no move to fight. He was apparently unaffected by his trip through the water.

The creature stood and stared at me without emotion. Then he spoke in that maddening, sing-song rhyme:

> *"For certain you're a funny thing;*
> *Dabble finds you interesting;*
> *Dabble offers you a task;*
> *Does one thing that you should ask."*

With that, the creature leaped behind him and disappeared into the earth. I sat there, stunned.

"What just happened?" I asked.

"You just did the most foolish thing I've ever seen anyone do. And got away with it." Django sat down with a thump and began to probe his cuts. "By all the saints, what on earth did you think you were doing?"

I shook my head. "I meant what I said. I'll see no one else die because of me."

"You poor, brave, gentle idiot. He can't die. He's a demon."

"A demon?"

"I thought you knew. He's a demon summoned by Radoul. If you hadn't saved him, he'd have sunk to the bottom, then burrowed out through the bottom and back to the surface."

I turned back to Django. "And if I hadn't saved him, what then? He'd still be trying to kill us, wouldn't he?"

Django shrugged. "I told you. Light and darkness. Your faith was greater than mine, you acted for no reason other than you felt it was the right thing to do." Django grinned wickedly. "And God has rewarded you by making the demon your friend."

"My pal, Dabble the demon."

Django winced as he laughed. The absurdity of having a demon for a buddy was too much. "Please, it hurts to laugh."

I sat there lost in the wonder of it all. "Mom, can my old chum Dabble spend the night? You'll like him.

We're just gonna shoot a few hoops, sacrifice a cat, drink some blood. Regular stuff."

Django rose carefully. "Come. I have some bandages back at the chamber, then we'll look elsewhere."

I got up, too. "Did he just grant me a wish?"

"Something like that, I think."

I closed my eyes. "I wish this was all over, we won, everybody's all right, and I'm back home." I opened my eyes and stared into the cells filled with the dead. "So much for the reliability of demons."

"Are you coming?" Django stood at the entrance to his tunnel.

"Wait a sec." I ran back and scooped up the rest of my stones, grabbed my slingshot, and ran back to Django. It was with a sinking feeling that I realized that somewhere in the château a werewolf—make that were-man—was looking to kill us, and I had shot my last silver bullet.

⌃18⌄

Despite all the blood, Django's wounds were fairly light. I helped him clean them up and wrapped the bandage around his wounded belly as best I could. He had a large bump on the noggin where Dabble had clobbered him, but only a small cut there which no longer bled.

As we moved back into the corridors it occurred to me that we would require water and food soon.

"How far to the other wing?" I asked.

"In distance, not much, but it is a winding, difficult way. These hidden passages were never designed for my convenience."

"I don't suppose you have any food socked away in here."

"I wish I did."

We came to a dead end in the passage, but a tight chimney rose above us. "Do as I do," Django said, and started up the tube of rock. His back pressed against one side as he braced himself with his thick legs. Slowly he worked his way upward. It didn't look too difficult, but I waited until he had a good start to follow. It took me a minute or two to get the knack, but once I had it I was faster than Django. I'd almost caught up as he reached the top.

He swung himself up and into a second passage, then reached his hand to me. I let him pull me in. We crawled about twenty yards before the passage opened enough to allow us to move at a crouching walk.

Django said, "Up ahead is a seep from the cistern above us. The water is pure, or at least it was in the days I served the Baron. There should be enough to ease our thirst."

It took perhaps ten minutes to reach the seep. The water pooled in a natural recess in the rock wall. Django drank first, then motioned that he thought the water was okay. I drank deeply. The frigid water was as fine a drink as I had ever known.

Django pulled a rag and dipped it in the water. "Try washing with this. You still stink from that pool below."

The odor wasn't bothering me anymore, but I washed anyway to make him happy. I heard a noise behind me, and turned in time to see hairy arms dragging Django through a hole in the wall.

"No!" I yelled and jumped after. I fell into a library. Django was wrestling with the wolf-man. Without thinking I waded into the middle of it. The wolf-man struck

96

me across the mouth. I flew across the room and slammed against a shelf with my back. Books tumbled onto me, and my vision blurred.

The wolf-man and Django continued to battle, ignoring me. I shook my head trying to clear it, and pushed the books off me. My right arm was hanging funny, and it was hard to move. I fumbled for my slingshot and the stones.

Even as I put a stone in the sling I knew that I could never pull it back with my arm. I cursed in frustration as the wolf-man rose leaving Django's body, unmoving, on the floor.

I threw the slingshot at the monster's head, diverting his attention for a moment. As those crimson eyes met mine I heard myself growling like an idiot, "Come on dog-man. Come and get it!"

I threw a book at him, and the wolf-man left Django for me. With an almost casual move it struck me backhanded. I spun, and slammed face first into the wall. Sharp pain exploded through my jaw and cheeks. I felt myself lifted in the air and hurled across the room. My arm broke with a loud crack as a wave of pain moved through my whole skeleton. Then it seemed to fade. I lay on the stone floor like a wet sack of beans. I was terrified. This never happened in the movies. How could I win after being so badly hurt? This was the real-world price of violence. I could no longer feel a thing, and I knew I must be in shock.

The room twirled around me. A low, muttering growl was the only sound as the wolf-man prowled around behind me.

He's killing off Django now, and then he'll come kill me, I thought. A rough hand grabbed me by the back of my shirt and lifted me. I was barely aware of Django dangling from the wolf-man's other hand.

My feet dragged along the floor as he hauled us out of the room. *So this is how it ends,* I thought. Somewhere along the way I passed out.

19

I floated in a forest filled with the scent of soft pines. A spirit moved gently across the forest floor, and an odd, distracted part of me recognized Sacajawea.

"It hurts," I whispered.

"It will hurt more," she said softly.

I turned my eyes. "We have lost."

"You are alive. You are the Chronicler."

"I'm a puddle of blood and broken meat in a castle in France."

"You must believe. You are the Chronicler. It all falls to you, now."

The smells were growing fainter. I was leaving. The spirit became ever more faint as I watched.

"It all falls to you," she chanted.

"Then, lady, we are up a creek," I said.

"What? You are delirious, boy. Snap out of it. There is no creek here."

"What?" I mumbled through broken lips. I looked

into the eyes of the most handsome man I'd ever seen. His smile was like the very sun. I tried to put my hand to my face, and realized my arms would not respond. Agony ripped through me, and I groaned.

The man continued to smile. "Delicious, isn't it? Pain, I mean." Through tears I watched him rise and walk over to the lump of bruised flesh that used to be Django. "And you, my little Hop-frog, do you suffer?"

He bent close as if to sniff the pain coming from Django. Nearby the wolf-man stood at hunched attention, his eyes staring blankly into the distance. The man gently assisted Django into a sitting position.

The sight of the poor soldier's bruised face took my breath away. One shoulder was shattered, and judging by the peculiar position of his legs, at least one was broken.

"Good, good," the man purred. "It's no fun when company falls asleep. And you are such a dear, old friend."

He rose and looked at me again.

"Who are you?" I muttered, hoarsely.

"Why, I'm your host." He stopped and made a sweeping bow. "Baron Radoul, at your service. What, are you disappointed? Were you expecting some wizened old man?"

I coughed and blood bubbled out of my mouth to dribble down my chin. The Baron frowned. "Oh, it does hurt so much to talk, doesn't it?" I worked my jaw,

100

and he nodded up and down as if trying to help. "What? You're wondering about your friend? Why he's right here." The Baron jumped forward and tilted my head back. I gasped.

Broccoli floated above us, encased in some kind of slimy cocoon. His features could just be made out through the translucent covering. To his right floated a sphere about the size of a softball. Light played from the sphere up and down the length of Broccoli as he floated. There was no sign of consciousness.

"Isn't it wonderful? I especially like the cocoon. An interesting little side effect, don't you think?" He smiled happily, obviously pleased with himself.

"I had despaired of ever finding the key to the orb's power, you know. It wasn't until my little wolf-friend arrived that I learned the key was coming to visit me. And thanks to your confiding in him, I know what I have to do later to make sure the Key gets back here. I must say, you've done me a tremendous service."

"You're welcome," I rasped.

"Hah! You see! That's another thing, this marvelous sense of humor you have. This incredible luck and drive. You evaded Dabble not once but twice! Extraordinary. Are you sure you're not a wizard?" He gazed at me expectantly.

"Positive."

"Amazing. But I'm sure you're anxious to see the result of all your trials. It wouldn't be fair of me to let you come all this way for nothing, would it?'' He turned to Django. ''Still with us, little Hop-frog? Look what your baron's got for you.''

With a flourish the Baron raised his arms and closed his eyes. Light flashed from the orb and centered on his hands, then shot in a vivid, green stream to Django.

The dwarf screamed as the light struck his battered form. ''The Protean Orb!'' shouted the Baron. ''Catalyst of change for all living things. I discovered it nearly two centuries ago. It took almost a hundred years to learn its first secrets. But I persevered.''

Django's body arched backward in a spine breaking curve as his legs thickened, swelled with the green light. His feet burst through soft sandals to splay across the floor.

''The ancient texts gave me clues, but never enough. My control was imperfect. Interesting results, yes, but failures, unfit to look after themselves. But I persevered for it was written that a key existed, and if it is written, it must be so. I could afford to wait.''

Django flipped forward again. His rear legs were huge, green spotted limbs. His head spread as his arms shrank inward. The eyes grew and bulged above his mouth. His mouth, too, changed, splitting open across his face nearly to each ear.

''You see how wonderful this is?'' The Baron's face was lit in an unholy joy as the sickening stream of light continued to batter change upon the dwarf. ''Now he is truly the Hop-frog, stronger, bigger, better than he has ever been. And my servant forever." The light shot off, and my heart dropped as Django sat contentedly before me, half man, half frog. His tongue fell from his mouth and landed, splat, upon the floor.

The Baron frowned. "Well, that's not right." He brightened. "But we can fix that later."

Anger filled me at the sight of my noble friend's humiliation.

I barely heard the Baron asking, "The question, my young friend, is who exactly *are* you?"

Who was I? Suddenly I knew. It came like some incredible leap of intuition. The clues were there if only they were looked at the right way!

"Who am I? Your worst nightmare." An evil grin spread across my ruined lips. I began to chuckle from deep inside. Pain roared over me as I laughed, but I could not stop. The Baron stamped his foot.

"What are you doing? What's wrong with you? Have you gone mad?"

I croaked. "You look like a little kid when you do that."

The Baron went dark with anger. "You mock me at your peril, child."

"I don't think so. You see, you've got it wrong. You thought Broccoli was the key to your orb, and in a sense he is. But he is more than that. The orb is only a part

103

of what is going on, and you, sir"—I coughed again—
"you, sir, don't count for very much at all."

"Rave on, fool. You should enjoy your life as a
magpie."

"Broccoli is not your key to the orb. Broccoli and
the orb are entwined. We were sent back not for you,
but to collect the orb. Poe and the orb are one!"

The Baron glanced up nervously at Broccoli, then
returned his stare to me. "And why should I believe
that?"

"Because I, Winston, am the one who tells you."

The Baron went to one knee, his face inches from
mine. His voice was low, dangerous. "And why, pray
tell, should that make a difference?"

"Because *I am the Chronicler and . . . it . . . is . . .
written!*"

There was a crack like a limb breaking, and the orb
suddenly dove toward Broccoli, losing itself, merging
with the body inside the cocoon. A dazzling show of
light blazed out from Broccoli's form and I had to turn
my head.

"No!" screamed the Baron. "I won't let you! Stop!"
A beam of sorcery, black and almost liquid with violence streamed toward the cocoon from the wizard's
hands, but a disc of energy immediately sprang into
being before it, blocking its force and sending it back
to its source. The Baron cried out before the charge of
it, and blasted backwards across the room.

104

The attack repelled, the cocoon returned to its business, ignoring the Baron. I was ready to pass out again, but I held on. The Baron glared a look of hatred at me from across the room. Slowly, he got to his feet.

He no longer looked so perfect. His face was twisted with hate, and the evil inside him showed clearly from his eyes. I should have been terrified, but instead I felt only cold anger.

"You will pay for this," he said, snarling, his hands held forward like claws. Power shot from his fingers, and I felt myself lifted in a current of sorcery. The beam swarmed across my body like a thousand bugs as it dangled me five feet above the floor.

"First, you will suffer as you've never suffered before. Then I will watch as my children eat you alive. What do you have to say to that, Chronicler?"

I twisted in agony, barely able to breathe. Yet still, I smiled grimly, and stared at the Baron, daring him until he looked me in the eye.

I whispered one word. "Dabble."

20

Dabble erupted through the floor and landed between the Baron and me. The Baron lost his concentration at the appearance of the demon, and I fell hard on the floor.

My body exploded with new waves of pain. It was an agony to work myself to a sitting position, but I managed it. It occurred to me that I was dying. So be it. I'd had enough of torment. It was almost over now.

"What does this mean? What is this treachery?" the Baron demanded.

Dabble only blinked, seemingly unconcerned by the Baron's rage.

"*I* summoned you! You are *my* servant!" the Baron whined.

"He serves the devil, you fool. Or himself. Or didn't you know he tried to kill Broccoli at Joan of Arc's camp?"

"He tried to kill you!"

"Sorry, errp, wrong!" I sang out like a game show

106

host. "The idea was to keep Broccoli away from the orb. But something changed. Broccoli went into the future. Broccoli got well, thinking the enchantment was yours. But that should not have worked. It was a demon's bite, and demons don't die. That means someone decided to let Broccoli reach the orb after all."

The Baron tottered, he put a hand to his face. "I know nothing of bites. I—I . . ."

"The devil decided to let you have your key, after all, knowing it would do you no good."

"But why? I have always been his servant. Why would he betray me?"

"Perhaps he owed another debt. Maybe you should have spent more time talking to your wolf-man."

Dabble turned to stare at Winston.

"Winston's smarter than he looks;
Something in that noggin cooks."

The Baron glared at Dabble. "Is this true? You've betrayed me for the sake of a wolf?"

Dabble shrugged.

"Truth can change from day to day;
That is what we demons say."

Around us lights continued to play on the walls as they glared out of the cocoon. Their intensity was

107

changing. Under the light's influence Django was changing back, slowly but surely, to the man he'd always
been. More light crept up the walls and fled through the
windows, searching for the things the orb had changed
before. Broccoli was gaining control, but he wasn't there
yet. I had to wrap this up before the Baron found a way
to hurt him.

The choice was taken from me. The Baron grabbed
me, and held me before him. Dabble watched without
emotion. I could barely think, and the room was taking
on a reddish tinge.

"You did this to me." He could barely speak. His
rage had changed him; the years were plain on him
now, and slime dribbled from his mouth. But he was
strong as an ox. He held me before him like a doll.
"You. Only you, and by all the devils of hell I will
have my revenge. And don't think you can fool me with
Dabble. You've already proved you can't kill anyone."
His hands closed around my throat.

I tried to speak, to have Dabble save me, but I could
not. The Baron began to squeeze. I squirmed feebly, my
strength gone. Then the pressure stopped. Through slit-
ted eyes I saw the Baron's face twisted in pain.

"Aaiiieee," he yelped, and again I fell to the floor.
From the corner of my eye I could see Django, his top
half once again changed to man-form, with his teeth
sunk deep into the Baron's thigh.

The Baron struck him once, twice, three times, and

108

Django fell away. The Blood Baron spun to me. He looked like a demon himself, now.

I breathed deep, summoned the last of my strength, and said softly, "Dabble, take him home with you. Forever."

The demon laughed, a high pitched giggle that sent shivers up my spine.

> *"It's sure he knows what wishing's for;*
> *Dabble likes him more and more."*

The room exploded in a blast of searing light, and chunks of cocoon rained around us like hail. The Baron screamed as a raging wind swept through the hall. Wood splintered banging against walls, and dust and blood caked my eyes.

I lay through it all without moving, my soul at peace. I watched the Baron, his face white with horror, as Dabble fell upon him and dragged him screaming down to hell.

Satisfied, I closed my eyes and died.

21

Ah, that forest. Of course, I didn't die, at least not yet. I found myself bobbing along in the piney green again, so I just waited for Sacajawea. Although I know now that I survived, I wasn't altogether sure at the time. Sacajawea appeared and smiled at me.

"Do you come here often?" I asked.

She laughed softly. "Always making jokes. You have acquitted yourself well, Chronicler."

I thought about that. "I have to admit, I'm pretty pleased with myself."

She chuckled. "As you should be. The forging of the Key is well begun."

"Begun? As in, more-to-come-later-because-we're-not-finished type begun?"

"You know the answer to that," she said quietly.

I thought for a minute. "Then I'm not dead?"

"Do you feel dead?"

"I've certainly felt more lively." I continued to float,

content to be away from my pain-wracked body. "I was right, wasn't I?"

"About what?" she asked, teasing.

"About . . . well, about everything, pretty much."

"Yes, you were right. It is part of your gift. You are the Chronicler. It is your gift—and curse—to see the truth, so that the truth may be written, that all may learn."

I felt lazy. I turned like a swimmer in the air exulting in the freedom. I looked and Sacajawea was walking away.

"But wait," I called. "What is to come? What shall we do?"

"I am a guide, not a prophet. Be true, Chronicler, be true!"

I opened my eyes to see stone. The air crackled with power and light. Django bent over me, then raised his head to look at someone.

"Save him," he said.

A wave of light spread over me, filling me with calm. I descended through the light to the very bits and pieces of my body. I rode along with T-cells through my bloodstream, watched the ease and knit of muscles damaged beyond repair, saw bones slide and move and fit, fusing at the broken joints without a sign of rupture. I saw my ribs return to their places, and watched a ragged hole in my lung close up and heal. I watched this strange parade of miracles, and thought, "It is good he does this now, for it will leave him soon."

My body sang with health and energy. Django smiled at me with a wacky grin, as if unable to believe our incredible luck.

Broccoli walked in a swirl of bright light. Throughout everything the wolf-man had sat motionless, enthralled to the Baron. Now Broccoli reached for him and said, "Tell us your story. Quickly."

The wolf-man licked his feral lips and shrugged. "There is little to tell. I was cursed years ago to walk as a man. I came because I'd heard there was a chance to lift the curse." His voice was eerie, a cross between a growl and a normal voice. "The closer we came, the more I wanted to leave your company. I feared you would spoil everything. But when I did leave, I passed Dabble and the others. I saw they meant to kill you, and I could not permit it. I owed you a life already. So I demanded payment from the demon."

Broccoli still shone, but his light was somewhat dimmer. It was obvious to everyone that the power was fading. "That is why I got well, because later you would demand the demon spare me."

Bienville shrugged. "Who can say? I demanded payment. He complied."

"Payment for what?" Broccoli asked.

"Centuries ago there was a child saved by a wolf. The devil's child. For that service, the devil owed a debt to wolves. What is promised to one is promised to all; what is promised by one, is honored by all. That is the way of the wolf.''

I heard myself gasp, ''The devil's child!''

''Aye,'' said the wolf-man.

''But you could have asked him to lift your own curse,'' I protested.

The wolf-man turned to me with sad eyes. ''I would not dishonor my kind with a selfish request.''

''Hurry,'' whispered Broccoli. ''Let me heal you, before it's gone.''

Broccoli held his hands out and grasped the wolf-man by its forelimbs. The light pulsed and ran from Broccoli to the creature. The wolf-man twisted his head in pain as his body began to shrink. All signs of manhood fled until at last a large, grey wolf stood proudly before us. Broccoli dropped to his knees, his energy spent. The wolf gently licked his face.

I heard a voice in my head. ''From this day forth, all of wolf-kind calls you friends. Should you ever need us we will come. What is promised by one is honored by all. It is the way of the wolf.'' Then it faded, and I shook my head as if from a dream. Was it real?

The wolf stared into my eyes with its own eyes of deep black. Suddenly it turned on its rear legs and leaped gracefully across the room and through the door.

I relaxed. There would now never be an Amber Man. Somewhere in England in my time were people who would live. I should have been pleased for them, but mostly I was pleased for Bienville.

"Run fast, brave wolf," I whispered.

Broccoli rose and smiled at me. "We did it, Winston. We really did it. If you had not come back . . ."

"Forget it," I said. "We're a team." The glow was all gone now. Broccoli looked like himself again. "How do you feel?"

"Good," he said. "The orb is . . ."—he felt at his chest and stomach as if searching for it—". . . gone somehow, but here. I don't know. It's peculiar. Like it's waiting now for something."

Django was peering down the hole through which Dabble had dragged the Baron.

"He is well and truly gone," he said. "It is hard to believe."

"What will you do now?" Broccoli asked him.

Django shook his head. "It is hard to know. First I must see that the people here get help. Now that the Baron is gone, the villagers will come forward, I think. And there are things in this château which must be disposed of before they fall into the wrong hands. There were many tools of mischief besides the orb."

Broccoli nodded. "I understand. Be wary, Django. Some of those tools may be dangerous."

"I hear you. But it must be done, and fate has apparently chosen me to do it. You have done us a great service, both of you."

114

"As you have done for us," said Broccoli. "Truly, the Maid of Orleans sacrificed much when she gave us you for a guide."

Django stepped forward and took Broccoli by his shoulders. "Tell me," he asked, his voice soft. "You are from the future. What of the Maid? Will she live? Will France be free?"

Broccoli looked at me nervously, but I remembered what I'd learned in history. I remembered the treachery and betrayal by the Dauphin, of a young maid humiliated before a court of wicked men, of cold cells, and years of deprivation and mistreatment, and—what was worst to her—a loss of faith. Until finally, her faith restored, that dear, brave woman died in the flames. All of England grew sick at heart to see the murder of such a noble creature by their leaders. It made me shiver.

Django's voice took on an edge of fear. "What do you see?"

"France will be free," I said quietly.

Django's face lit with joy. "Praise God!" He embraced Broccoli in a bear hug, and I watched Broccoli's face go red. I gave him a weak grin.

The dwarf stepped back and smiled at both of us. "God bless the day He brought you to us. So tell me, will you stay? Will you help us?"

"We cannot," I said, before Broccoli got any more noble ideas. "Our work here is done, as some hero somewhere once said."

"Well, Winston?" Broccoli asked, stepping forward as he fiddled with his time belt. "Are you ready to go home?"

I nodded. Django crushed me in a hug, and I told him goodbye. Broccoli set my belt as well, and then pushed the button. The room disappeared as I walked through the cabinet into Broccoli's house.

22

Broccoli and I sat in his living room saying nothing. We had been home a few hours, and both of us were sort of spent by the adventure. I thought I might have to take time to clean up, but Broccoli's healing had gone farther than my body. It had cleaned my clothes and rid me of that sewer smell I'd gained in the dungeons. So there was nothing to do but vegetate.

Finally I said, "What about when I came back? I mean, if I go home now, will I find myself waiting there?"

"Did you find yourself there before?" he asked.

"No."

"Then you won't now. One of the things I've learned is time doesn't permit those kinds of paradoxes. And if you think about them too much it just drives you crazy. For instance—"

I interrupted. "For instance, since we stopped the Wizard, there is no Amber Man, and therefore we never had a reason to go at all and so we didn't go, right?"

"Except we did. That kind of paradox time allows, but it only allows it to us, because we were the participants. In effect, we have a set of memories no one else has."

I grunted. "Great. That makes me feel so much better."

A few more minutes passed. Broccoli said, "Do you want a soda or something?"

"No. Say, what time is it, anyway? When are your folks due in?"

Broccoli looked away. "I don't know."

Since I was the Chronicler, maybe I should have had a big blast of insight right then about Broccoli's parents, but it didn't happen. Not then, anyway.

"You don't know what time it is, or you don't know when your folks are due?"

"Neither one. There's a clock in the kitchen, over the sink."

I went into the kitchen and saw that it was 4:30.

"Oh no," I yelled. "Mom's home." I stuck my head back in the living room. "Gotta go, Broccoli. Mom's home." He had an odd look on his face, but I didn't pay a lot of attention as I raced out the back door and across my yard to the house.

Mom was putting the wash in the dryer as I walked in. She straightened to look at me. "Well! So where have you been? Didn't you read my note? I asked you to move the washing, and you didn't."

118

"I'm sorry, Mom. I forgot."

"That's no excuse. And there's no excuse for being out all day without me knowing where you were, either. Why didn't you leave a note saying where you'd gone?"

"Aww, I was just next door, Mom. With Broccoli."

Her brow creased, and she bent forward a little as if she couldn't hear.

"With who?"

"Broccoli. He's the new kid next door."

That helped a little. She wasn't frowning now, and I could see she was curious about our new neighbors.

"I didn't know there were any children your age over there," she said.

"Just him. Can he come to dinner?"

"Is it okay with his parents?"

"Oh sure," I said, lying through my teeth. "They had to go out, and they won't be back until really late." I ran my hand over the dryer nonchalantly. "It's a pretty big old house. I'll bet he gets pretty scared over there by himself."

I followed Mom back into the kitchen. She opened the refrigerator and stood staring inside like an unhappy general reviewing poor soldiers.

"Maybe we should ask him if he wants to spend the night. If it's okay with his parents."

"Gee, Mom. What a good idea. I'll ask him."

"Oh?" she asked, smiling. "You mean you didn't already have this all set up?"

I held my hand to my chest in a "Who? Me?" pose and she laughed.

"Yeah, you're about as subtle as a cannon. You can ask him over, but—"

"Yay!" I yelled and started out the door.

"But *first*," she said, raising her voice, "you will clean that room of yours. And I mean clean it. Don't just shove everything in the closet."

"Yes ma'am," I said resignedly. I climbed the stairs like a condemned man on his way to the gallows. It took me almost forty minutes to clean my room. From time to time I stopped and looked over at Poe's house, but I never saw him moving around in there.

When everything was done I ran downstairs.

"Dinner in thirty minutes," Mom said as I ran by. "Tell him it's pork chops," she shouted after me.

I found Broccoli still sitting on the couch. He looked surprised to see me.

"Did you forget something?" he asked.

"Nah, just you. You wanna spend the night at my house?"

"Why?" he asked. His face had this strange look, half hope and half fear. It made me feel funny. In all the time I'd known him he'd seemed so in control, like he knew everything about everybody. Now he looked kind of like a puppy who expects to be hurt.

120

"What kind of question is that?" I asked. "Do you want to stay here by yourself all night? After everything we just went through, I don't know, I just thought it would be nice to have some company. I'm still not quite over being scared, you know?"

Broccoli looked angry. "What makes you think my parents won't be here? Why, they're due—"

"No they're not. They're not due tonight or this week or this month or even this year are they? Where are they, Broccoli?" Now that I'd made the guess it seemed obvious to me.

Broccoli stared at me, and then his chin began to tremble. Tears formed, and ran down his cheeks. "I don't know," he whimpered. "I can't find them."

Then he really began to cry. I couldn't help but wonder how long he'd been holding it in. Huge, strangling sobs came out of him, and I didn't know what to do. I just sat there like an idiot so he wouldn't have to cry alone.

After a while he began to calm down.

"What happened to them?"

"I don't know. They went to work just like always right after they bought this house, but before we moved in. Maybe three months ago. They'd never left me alone for more than two days before. I tried everything to track them down, but I couldn't find them. Then the men from Time came and moved us. I asked them where

121

my parents were, but they wouldn't talk. They told me I had to move, and I had to just have faith.

"So, I've been trying to find other things to keep me busy."

"Like the Amber Man," I said.

"Yeah, like that." He looked at me. "You see, I'm not like other kids—"

"No kidding." He looked hurt, and I added, "I'm sorry. Go on."

"I'm *supposed* to be able to look after myself. My folks know that I talk to spirits and study magic. They encourage it. It was never easy for me to make friends. Other kids always thought I was weird. But you get used to that. You expect it because you have your parents and you have the things that really interest you and usually that's enough."

"You didn't have any friends?"

"I didn't need any friends. Who was I going to make friends with? Then this all came up, dreaming about the Wizard, about being the Key."

"I had those dreams, too."

Broccoli nodded. "I know. We are linked together. I know that now in a way I didn't before." He looked at me with sadness in his eyes. "Just as I know that my parents being gone has something to do with the forging of the Key. Me." His chin starting shaking again. "But I miss them."

I stood up, and put my hand on his shoulder. "That's

a tough break, Broccoli. But I promise you, we will find them. Sooner or later, we will find them, and bring them home for you.''

''You mean that?''

''I am the Chronicler, aren't I? I say it is written, and therefore, it must be so. I just don't know how yet, or when. But I can feel it. It's right.''

Broccoli smiled a little. I clapped his shoulder.

''Just as I can see that we are due for some pork chops, so go wash your face and grab your p.j.s.''

I waited while Broccoli gathered a few things. Together we walked out the back door and back to my house. It was a lot to think about. Where were Broccoli's parents? What did their disappearance have to do with anything? And to *what* was Broccoli the Key?

I didn't envy Broccoli his problems, even though it looked like some of them would end up being mine as well. I wondered if I would be able to put up as good a front if my Mom and Dad weren't there to help me. But I knew one thing. This adventure, this testing we had embarked upon, was the most astonishing and important thing to happen in my life. And if Broccoli needed me, I wasn't going to let him down.

Mom smiled at us as we walked in.

''Well, who have we here?'' she asked, smiling.

''This is Brock Lee Poe, Mom. He's my best friend.''

Broccoli smiled broadly for the first time since I'd known him.

I knew there were lots of troubles ahead, mysteries yet to be solved. But for that night we could just be pals like anybody else, and save our troubles for another day.

Later Mom brought out a Ouija Board game. Broccoli politely said, no thanks, and asked me to teach him to play Nintendo.

So endeth Chronicle One
of the Forging of the Key

Don't miss more scary adventures
with Winston and Broccoli in
VAMPIRE MOM,
coming in August 1995 from Avon Camelot.
Check out the following preview . . .

Broccoli and I went with my mother to the flea market south of town. People from all over our part of the state came to sell whatever they could gather and display. It may sound boring, but it's actually pretty cool, almost like a fair. Booths filled with bright-colored cloths and smooth, burnished woodcrafts delight the eye, as shoppers laugh and bustle through, only stopping to haggle with the tradesmen. Food stands are everywhere, offering barbecue sandwiches, fat sausages, and roasted ears of corn slathered with butter.

Mom paid our way in and turned to us. "Well, boys, what are you going to do?"

"We figure we'd go check out the comic books," I said. Mr. Ferguson kept a stand stocked with tattered books and magazines—great stuff—some from all the way back in the 1950's. They were expensive, but money wasn't really a problem when you knew Broccoli.

Mom looked at her watch. I noticed one or two men glancing at her as they walked by. I grinned to myself. Dad pretended to be jealous at the way men were always looking at Mom, but we all knew that secretly he was proud of her beauty, and not a little amazed that he was the man she loved. Today she wore a t-shirt under a light sweater, blue jeans, and tennis shoes.

Mom had never been real big on appearances. She wore almost no makeup. She did not even like to paint her nails unless she was going out for a fancy evening. Mom kept them short at all times because, as she said, she'd just bite them off if they grew long anyway. But despite her simple clothes and plain fixings, she looked as pretty as a movie star. Well, at least I thought so.

"Give it forty-five minutes," she said. "Then I want you two to come looking for me. You can cover a lot more ground than I can. I want to be home in time to start dinner. Think you can remember that?"

"Aww, Mom," I said.

"We'll remember," said Broccoli. He tugged at my sleeve. "Come on, let's go see what old man Ferguson's got."

"Bye," I shouted, running after Broccoli.

On the way to Ferguson's we passed a strange setup. A gaunt man with thin blond hair glared at us from behind a card table heaped high with junk. Beyond him a girl with dirty, stringy hair sat in a metal folding chair. She stared down at a Nintendo Game Boy held in her lap. A run-down station wagon squatted on blown shocks nearby, its rear doors open. The car had been cut and rebuilt to feature a tilting shanty on its back half. It looked like the man and girl lived in it.

Broccoli put a hand on my arm as we passed. "There's something about that guy . . ." he muttered.

Indeed, the man stared at us as if we were sworn enemies. I felt a chill as his ice blue eyes burned into mine. As I turned away I saw the girl staring at us, too. But there was no hate in her eyes. There was nothing at all. You'd find more expression in the eyes of a Barbie doll. It made me shiver.

At Ferguson's we quickly forgot about the odd pair as we lost ourselves in the stacks of old *Fantastic Four, Silver Surfer,* and *Avenger* comics. Piles of pulp magazines with names like *Amazing Stories, Weird Tales,* and *Black Mask* dominated one corner. The center of the booth held a long table heaped with used paperbacks.

"You know," I whispered, "we could always go back in time and buy all this stuff new."

Broccoli looked at me in honest surprise. "Where would the fun of collecting be in that?"

I laughed and continued scrounging. Ferguson watched us for a while, then went to the front of the stand. He shook his head and began fussing with old paperbacks on the table. I wondered what his problem was. Usually he talked our ears off. He was proud of

129

his inventory and delighted to meet anyone who shared his love of old books, especially if they were children.

"Are you all right, Mr. Ferguson?" I asked.

"Eh? All right? Yes, yes, sure I am. Just have the fidgets today, that's all." He walked to the front again and glanced back the way we'd walked in. Broccoli and I exchanged knowing looks.

"Some people . . ." Ferguson mumbled as he returned behind his counter.

"It's that man with the house-car, isn't it?" guessed Broccoli.

"Eh? No, No. Well, yes, dang it! I don't like it. Got a nice bunch of folks comes here to dicker, and that feller, well, there's just somethin' wrong." Ferguson leaned forward. "Went by to say howdy and welcome, and that man give me a look like I'd just spit in his oatmeal. Me, who never bothered nobody. It's a bad sign, I tell you. That kind can ruin a market like we got here. Soon we'll start gettin' all those grifters sellin' smuggled birds from Mexico, and—well, and other things."

He meant drugs. A flea market two counties over had a problem last year with people trying to sell dope to kids.

Our conversation stopped as the girl with the stringy hair walked in. She came right up to me as if she knew me and gave me the Game Boy.

"What the—" I started, but she was already walking

130

away. I ran up to her and caught her by her shoulder. I tried to put the Game Boy back in her hands, but she refused to hold it. She wore no expression, merely stood there as I tried to make her take it.

"Wait a minute," Broccoli said. He gazed into her eyes as if trying to read something in them. No one spoke for a moment. Finally he asked, "Why?"

The girl flinched, her eyes shifting back and forth at lightning speed. She moved away from Broccoli and grabbed Mr. Ferguson by the hands. Slowly, she began to tremble. Mr. Ferguson turned beet red, his eyes glazed, and an unearthly voice drooled from between his slack lips.

"The Key must not be thwarted."

Again silence came over us as the girl released the old man and walked away, her face expressionless. I stood dumbfounded with the Game Boy in my hands. Not knowing what else to do, I put it in my jacket pocket. Mr Ferguson sat down, wiping sweat from his forehead.

"Somebody tell me what just happened," he said.

Broccoli had followed her outside, pointing. "Look," he said, his voice fearful.

I joined him and watched as my mother let that awful man place a necklace around her throat. An eerie chuckle floated through the air to us. Mom stepped away from the table and wavered, almost falling. She moved her head back and forth, as if trying to shake something out of her ear. Finally she stopped and began to walk, her steps growing more firm with every moment. By the time we reached her she was walking normally. An evil smile played across her lips.

The man at the table looked around in bewilderment, as if he'd been asleep all day and suddenly awakened in a strange place. His sullen, strange expression had vanished and was replaced by a new look of confusion. Behind him stood the girl, her face as empty as ever.

"Hello boys. Do you like my new necklace. See the stone? It's garnet, my birthstone."

Mom's voice seemed the same, but her eyes, dear God, her eyes were not her own.

"Mom?" My voice was tiny, almost whining.

Her eyes glinted like sparks from flint. "Oh yes, it's Mom. And you are Winston, Mommy's little man."

I shuddered as she spoke. She seemed so—foreign. Not Mom but some kind of mother-thing. I could almost see it in there, whatever possessed her, hiding within her eyes, laughing at me.

"Now come, boys. Mommy has a big surprise planned for you." Her tongue licked her lips. "A big surprise, and there is still so much left to do."

Her hands reached out for me. The nails were long and pointed, each as red as a drop of blood.

IF YOU DARE TO BE SCARED...
READ SPINETINGLERS!
by M.T. COFFIN

THE SUBSTITUTE CREATURE
77829-7/$3.50 US/$4.50 Can

Everyone knows about substitute teachers. When they show up it's time for fun and games. That's why no one believes Jace's crazy story about seeing the new substitute, Mr. Hiss, in the men's room...smearing blood all over his hands and face!

BILLY BAKER'S DOG WON'T STAY BURIED
77742-8/$3.50 US/$4.50 Can

Billy Baker's dog Howard has come back from the dead...bringing all his friends from the pet cemetery. Every night, long-dead cats and dogs dig themselves out of their graves in search of people who bullied and beat them, locked them up or tied them down. Now it's their turn to get even!

LOOK FOR THESE OTHER TERRIFYING TALES
COMING SOON

MY TEACHER'S A BUG
77785-1/$3.50 US/$4.50 Can

WHERE HAVE ALL THE PARENTS GONE?
78117-4/$3.50 US/$4.50 Can

Buy these books at your local bookstore or use this coupon for ordering:
....
Mail to: Avon Books, Dept BP, Box 767, Rte 2, Dresden, TN 38225   C
Please send me the book(s) I have checked above.
❑ My check or money order— no cash or CODs please— for $_____ is enclosed
(please add $1.50 to cover postage and handling for each book ordered— Canadian residents
add 7% GST).
❑ Charge my VISA/MC Acct#_____Exp Date_____
Minimum credit card order is two books or $6.00 (please add postage and handling charge of
$1.50 per book — Canadian residents add 7% GST). For faster service, call
1-800-762-0779. Residents of Tennessee, please call 1-800-633-1607. Prices and numbers
are subject to change without notice. Please allow six to eight weeks for delivery.

Name_____
Address_____
City_____State/Zip_____
Telephone No._____   MTC 0495

From Award-Winning Author

WILL HOBBS

Bearstone

71249-0/$3.50 US/$4.25 Can
(An ALA Best Book)
High in the mountains of Colorado,
Cloyd renames himself Lone Bear and
discovers the power of his brave heritage.

Beardance

72317-4/$3.99 US/$4.99 Can
(An ALA Best Book)
"As compelling as *Bearstone*!"
School Library Journal

The Big Wander

72140-6/$3.99 US/$4.99 Can

Changes in Latitudes

71619-4/$3.50 US/$4.25 Can

Buy these books at your local bookstore or use this coupon for ordering:
....
Mail to: Avon Books, Dept BP, Box 767, Rte 2, Dresden, TN 38225   C
Please send me the book(s) I have checked above.
❏ My check or money order— no cash or CODs please— for $_____is enclosed
(please add $1.50 to cover postage and handling for each book ordered— Canadian residents
add 7% GST).
❏ Charge my VISA/MC Acct#_____Exp Date_____
Minimum credit card order is two books or $6.00 (please add postage and handling charge of
$1.50 per book — Canadian residents add 7% GST). For faster service, call
1-800-762-0779. Residents of Tennessee, please call 1-800-633-1607. Prices and numbers
are subject to change without notice. Please allow six to eight weeks for delivery.

Name_____
Address_____
City_____State/Zip_____
Telephone No._____   WH 0295

Stories of Adventure From
THEODORE TAYLOR
Bestselling Author of THE CAY

STRANGER FROM THE SEA: TEETONCEY
71024-2/$3.99 US/$4.99 Can

Ben O'Neal spotted a body on the sand—a girl of about ten or eleven; almost his own age—half drowned, more dead than alive. The tiny stranger he named Teetoncey would change everything about the way Ben felt about himself.

BOX OF TREASURES: TEETONCEY AND BEN O'NEAL
71025-0/$3.99 US/$4.99 Can

Teetoncey had not spoken a word in the month she had lived with Ben and his mother. But then the silence ends and Teetoncey reveals a secret about herself and the *Malta Empress* that will change their lives forever.

INTO THE WIND: THE ODYSSEY OF BEN O'NEAL
71026-9/$3.99 US/$4.99 Can

At thirteen, Ben O'Neal is about to begin his lifelong dream—to go to sea. But before Ben sails, he receives an urgent message from Teetoncey, saying she's in trouble.

Buy these books at your local bookstore or use this coupon for ordering:

Mail to: Avon Books, Dept BP, Box 767, Rte 2, Dresden, TN 38225   C
Please send me the book(s) I have checked above.
❑ My check or money order— no cash or CODs please— for $_____is enclosed
(please add $1.50 to cover postage and handling for each book ordered— Canadian residents add 7% GST).
❑ Charge my VISA/MC Acct#_____Exp Date_____
Minimum credit card order is two books or $6.00 (please add postage and handling charge of $1.50 per book — Canadian residents add 7% GST). For faster service, call 1-800-762-0779. Residents of Tennessee, please call 1-800-633-1607. Prices and numbers are subject to change without notice. Please allow six to eight weeks for delivery.

Name_____
Address_____
City_____State/Zip_____
Telephone No._____   TEE 0195

Avon Camelot Presents
Award-Winning Author

THEODORE TAYLOR

THE CAY 00142-X $3.99 US/$4.99 Can

After being blinded in a fatal shipwreck, Phillip was rescued from the shark-infested waters by the kindly old black man who had worked on deck. Cast up on a remote island, together they began an amazing adventure.

THE TROUBLE WITH TUCK 62711-6/ $3.99 US/$4.99 Can

Twice Helen's dog Tuck had saved her life. And when she discovered he was going blind, she fought to become his eyes— now it was her turn to save *his* life.

TUCK TRIUMPHANT 71323-3/ $3.99 US/$4.99 Can

At last...the miracle dog returns in the heartwarming sequel to *The Trouble with Tuck*.

MARIA 72120-1/ $3.99 US/ $4.99 Can

THE MALDONADO MIRACLE 70023-9/$3.99 US/$4.99 Can

Buy these books at your local bookstore or use this coupon for ordering:

Mail to: Avon Books, Dept BP, Box 767, Rte 2, Dresden, TN 38225 C
Please send me the book(s) I have checked above.
❑ My check or money order— no cash or CODs please— for $_____is enclosed (please add $1.50 to cover postage and handling for each book ordered— Canadian residents add 7% GST).
❑ Charge my VISA/MC Acct#_____Exp Date_____
Minimum credit card order is two books or $6.00 (please add postage and handling charge of $1.50 per book — Canadian residents add 7% GST). For faster service, call 1-800-762-0779. Residents of Tennessee, please call 1-800-633-1607. Prices and numbers are subject to change without notice. Please allow six to eight weeks for delivery.

Name_____
Address_____
City_____State/Zip_____
Telephone No._____ TAY 1194

From out of the Shadows...
Stories Filled With Mystery
and Suspense by

MARY DOWNING HAHN

THE TIME OF THE WITCH
71116-8/ $3.99 US/ $4.99 Can

STEPPING ON THE CRACKS
71900-2/ $3.99 US/ $4.99 Can

THE DEAD MAN IN INDIAN CREEK
71362-4/ $3.99 US/ $4.99 Can

THE DOLL IN THE GARDEN
70865-5/ $3.50 US/ $4.25 Can

FOLLOWING THE MYSTERY MAN
70677-6/ $3.99 US/ $4.99 Can

TALLAHASSEE HIGGINS
70500-1/ $3.99 US/ $4.99 Can

WAIT TILL HELEN COMES
70442-0/ $3.50 US/ $4.25 Can

THE SPANISH KIDNAPPING DISASTER
71712-3/ $3.99 US/ $4.99 Can

Coming Soon
TIME FOR ANDREW
72469-3/$3.99 US/$4.99 Can

DAPHNE'S BOOK
72355-7/$3.99 US/$4.99 Can

Buy these books at your local bookstore or use this coupon for ordering:
....
Mail to: Avon Books, Dept BP, Box 767, Rte 2, Dresden, TN 38225   C
Please send me the book(s) I have checked above.
❏ My check or money order— no cash or CODs please— for $_____is enclosed
(please add $1.50 to cover postage and handling for each book ordered— Canadian residents
add 7% GST).
❏ Charge my VISA/MC Acct#_____Exp Date_____
Minimum credit card order is two books or $6.00 (please add postage and handling charge of
$1.50 per book — Canadian residents add 7% GST). For faster service, call
1-800-762-0779. Residents of Tennessee, please call 1-800-633-1607. Prices and numbers
are subject to change without notice. Please allow six to eight weeks for delivery.

Name_____
Address_____
City_____State/Zip_____
Telephone No._____   MDH 0195

Join in the Wild and Crazy Adventures with Some Trouble-Making Plants

by Nancy McArthur

THE PLANT THAT ATE DIRTY SOCKS
75493-2/ $3.99 US/ $4.99 Can

THE RETURN OF THE PLANT THAT ATE DIRTY SOCKS
75873-3/ $3.50 US/ $4.25 Can

THE ESCAPE OF THE PLANT THAT ATE DIRTY SOCKS
76756-2/ $3.50 US/ $4.25 Can

THE SECRET OF THE PLANT THAT ATE DIRTY SOCKS
76757-0/ $3.50 US/ $4.50 Can

MORE ADVENTURES OF THE PLANT THAT ATE DIRTY SOCKS
77663-4/ $3.50 US/ $4.50 Can

Buy these books at your local bookstore or use this coupon for ordering:

Mail to: Avon Books, Dept BP, Box 767, Rte 2, Dresden, TN 38225   C
Please send me the book(s) I have checked above.
❑ My check or money order— no cash or CODs please— for $_____is enclosed
(please add $1.50 to cover postage and handling for each book ordered— Canadian residents
add 7% GST).
❑ Charge my VISA/MC Acct#_____Exp Date_____
Minimum credit card order is two books or $6.00 (please add postage and handling charge of
$1.50 per book — Canadian residents add 7% GST). For faster service, call
1-800-762-0779. Residents of Tennessee, please call 1-800-633-1607. Prices and numbers
are subject to change without notice. Please allow six to eight weeks for delivery.

Name_____
Address_____
City_____State/Zip_____
Telephone No._____   ESC 1294